Goosebumps®

HOW I LEARNED TO FLY

R. L. STINE

SCHOLASTIC INC.
New York Toronto London Auckland Sydney
Mexico City New Delhi Hong Kong Buenos Aires

ISBN 0-439-79620-2

The *Goosebumps* book series created by Parachute Press, Inc.
Published by Scholastic Inc.
SCHOLASTIC, GOOSEBUMPS,
and associated logos are trademarks and/or registered
trademarks of Scholastic Inc.

12 11 10 9 8 7 6 5   7 8 9 10 11/0

Printed in the U.S.A.   40

HOW I LEARNED TO FLY

The day I learned how to fly, I was worried about Wilson Schlamme.

I spend a lot of time worrying about Wilson. I've always had trouble with that guy.

Do you know why?

He thinks he's better than me — and I know he isn't.

I'm Jack Johnson. And I'm not the kind of kid who likes to enter contests. Really. I don't like to compete.

I always let my dad win at chess. Just because it means so much to him to win. And I even let my dog Morty win our wrestling matches on the living room floor.

But Wilson never gives me a break. He always has to prove that he's the best at everything.

If I'm chewing bubble gum, he tries to blow bigger bubbles. When my bubble is twice as big as Wilson's, he says that his is rounder!

If my bubble is bigger — *and* rounder — he

sticks his finger in mine and pops it all over my face.

He's trouble, that guy. Real trouble.

Especially when Mia Montez is around.

Mia is the cutest girl at Malibu Middle School. Ask anybody. Everything about Mia is cute.

She has big green eyes and a perfect, little nose. I think Mia's nose is the first thing I noticed about her. I really admired that nose. I guess that's because my nose is kind of big.

And Mia has the prettiest hair. Short, straight black hair. Really shiny. My hair is dark — like Mia's — but it's curly. Way too curly.

Know what Mia is totally crazy about? Hearts. It sort of makes sense. She was born on Valentine's Day.

She wears a heart necklace every day to school. And a charm bracelet with lots of silver and gold hearts dangling from it.

On her right hand, she wears a ruby red heart ring. And she has earrings that match. She looks so *cute* in all those hearts.

Anyway, when Mia is around, that's when Wilson is at his worst! He has to show off in front of her. And he has to prove that he's better than me.

Wilson likes to compete. Wilson likes to win.

So what choice do I have? I have to show Wilson that he's wrong. I have to prove that I'm as good as he is. I don't want Mia to think I'm a loser.

"Jack, can I borrow your eraser?" My friend Ethan Polke tapped me on the shoulder. Ethan sits behind me during free period in school. He never has erasers. He's always losing them.

"Sure." I turned around and handed him the new one I bought yesterday. Because he lost my old one the day before.

I hardly use my eraser anyway. At least not when I'm drawing superheroes.

I love to draw superheroes. And I'm really good at it. I never have to fix a single line.

"Hey — that's awesome!" Ethan pointed over my shoulder to my sketch of The Incredible Laser Man.

The Incredible Laser Man is my newest superhero. I draw superheroes every day. In the morning before I go to school. During free period. And at night after I finish my homework. And then, when I go to bed, I dream about them.

One day I'm going to be a comic book artist. I have a folder at home packed with my superhero drawings. The Fearless Falcon. Shadow Boy. The Masked Mantis. They're all going to be famous one day. I know it.

I studied my sketch of The Incredible Laser Man. He wore a really cool jumpsuit. His huge muscles bulged against the tight material.

A powerful lightning bolt streaked across his

massive chest. Two more lightning bolts zig-zagged down his muscular legs.

I drew a pair of mysterious black goggles to hide his eyes — so no one would know his true identity. I didn't know it either, yet.

First I draw the character — then I make up the story.

The Incredible Laser Man held his mighty arms up to the sky. I started to draw laser beams shooting from his fingertips. The bell rang just as I finished.

I jumped up from my seat. I couldn't wait to show The Incredible Laser Man to Mia. She was going to love it!

"Hey, Mia!" I held my drawing out to her. "Want to see my —"

"Out of my way, *Jackie*." I turned and saw Wilson. He was carrying a drawing too. He shoved me hard from behind.

I fell over Mia's desk. My drawing flew from my hand and fluttered to the floor.

"Thank you, Wilson!" Mia held Wilson's drawing in her hand. She flashed him a big smile. "Look at this, Jack. Look what Wilson drew."

I glanced over Mia's shoulder. Wilson had drawn a *team* of superheroes. FIVE of them. Colored in.

In sparkly letters at the top he had written: MIA'S PROTECTORS.

Yuck.

"Look what *Jackie* drew!" Wilson cried. He snatched my drawing from the floor.

"Wilson, don't call me Jackie!" I declared. "I told you a million times, I really hate being called that."

"Sorry. I forgot." Wilson smirked. "I won't do it again — *Jackie*."

I glared at Wilson. "Give me back my drawing!" I snapped. I reached out for it. But Wilson was too fast for me. He shoved it in front of Mia's face.

"It's The Incredible Lazy Man!" he hooted.

Mia giggled at his dumb joke.

I wanted to disappear.

"It's very cute, Jack," Mia said, handing it back to me. Then she and Wilson slipped on their backpacks and headed outside.

Okay — so Mia liked Wilson's drawing better. No big deal, I told myself. I stuffed my drawing into my backpack.

Just wait until we get outside.

Just wait until Mia sees my new twenty-one-speed Silver Streak racing bike.

She's going to love it!

I ran outside — just in time to see Mia circling my new bike. "Cool!" she said, trying to catch her reflection in the handlebars. "Maybe I'll ask Mom and Dad for a bike like this for my birthday."

I knew Mia would be impressed.

"You don't want *that* for your birthday," Wilson snickered. "You want *this*!"

Wilson pointed to *his* new bike.

His new heavy-duty dirt bike.

"Oh, wow!" Mia exclaimed. "WOW!"

My stomach twisted into a knot.

"I don't like those skinny racing bikes," Wilson sneered, shaking his head at my bike. "Too flimsy. I like a REAL bike."

I was so steamed! I wanted to take his big dirt bike and ride it back and forth over Wilson's head.

My new bike was awesome. It wasn't flimsy at all.

Why did everything have to be a contest? And why did Wilson always win?

Little did I know as the three of us rode home that the contest was only beginning!

2

"I win!" Wilson shouted, jumping off his bike. He leaned it against the tree in front of my house. He pumped his fists in the air. "The Silver Snail comes in second!" he announced as I rode up, drenched in sweat.

"Great race, guys," Mia said, pedaling up to us.

I wanted to ride home from school next to Mia. But Wilson wanted to race — and Mia thought it was a cool idea.

The hills of Malibu are awesome for racing. They wind around and around. I love to climb those hills on my bike, then go speeding down. And I'm really great at taking some of the sharp turns.

I gripped the handlebars of my bike.

I was confident.

I had twenty-one speeds.

We raced.

Wilson won.

I leaned my bike next to Wilson's, trying to

catch my breath. Morty, my rust-colored cocker spaniel, trotted out from the backyard to greet us.

"Hey, Morty!" The hearts on Mia's bracelet clinked softly as she scratched Morty's neck. Morty likes Mia as much as I do. His tail wagged like crazy. He jumped up to lick her face. Then he started on me.

"Whoa. Here comes Wilson's dog." Mia pointed across the street to Wilson's house. Wilson's enormous Labrador charged full speed toward us.

"Down, boy." Wilson laughed as his dog leaped up on him. He nearly knocked Wilson over.

"Terminator is TWICE as big as Morty," Wilson bragged to Mia.

"But Morty is smarter," I boasted. "We taught Morty to carry his food dish to the sink when he's finished eating."

"That's pretty smart," Mia agreed.

"You call that smart?" Wilson sneered. "We taught Terminator to answer the phone when we're not home."

"That's definitely smarter," Mia said. "That is really, really smart."

"That's not so smart," I argued. "Morty can roll over and —"

"Oh, noooo!"

We all heard a cry.

Mrs. Green, my next-door neighbor, poked her

head out of her front door and screamed. She stared in horror at the tree across the street. The tree in front of Wilson's house.

There was Olive — Mrs. Green's new kitten — sitting on the edge of a high tree limb. Her fur stood on end. Her little body shook. She let out a soft whimper.

"Oh, poor Olive!" Mia cried. "She's going to fall! Someone has to save her!"

"I will!" Wilson and I shouted together.

Oh, no, you won't, Wilson! I thought. You're not going to win this time.

With a burst of speed, I raced across the street. My sneakers pounded the sidewalk. I reached the tree first!

"Give me a boost," I ordered Wilson. Before he could argue, I wrapped my arms around the tree trunk and raised my foot. Wilson gave me a boost.

I inched my way up the trunk. I gazed out — over the hilltops. My eyes followed their winding path down, down, down. Right down to the beach. The beach stretched along the coast for miles.

I glanced down and smiled at Mia.

"Hurry, Jack!" she cried nervously.

"Don't worry, Mia," I declared. "I'm on my way!"

Yes! I am on my way to save Olive. And you're *not*, Wilson.

I climbed higher and higher — until I reached the limb where Olive sat. Her whole body shivered with fright. She let out a terrified squeak when she spotted me.

I studied the tree limb. It was very slender.

I didn't know if it would hold my weight.

"What are you waiting for, Jackie?" Wilson shook the tree trunk. "I'll come up and get her if you're afraid."

Ha! No way, Wilson!

I crawled out on the limb. Very slowly.

Olive whimpered.

I stopped.

I crawled out some more.

Olive inched away from me.

I stopped again.

Olive stared into my eyes. Then she lifted her front paws — to jump!

Down below, I could hear Mrs. Green and Mia gasp.

"No, Olive," I begged softly. "Stay."

I moved a little closer — close enough to grab her now.

I slowly reached out to her.

My fingertips brushed against her soft fur.

Then my knee slipped off the branch. I lost my balance. I lurched to the left.

"Noooo!"

I let out a shrill cry as I dropped from the tree.

3

I shot my arms up. I groped frantically for the tree limb.

And missed.

My stomach flopped as I plunged down. Down.

I closed my eyes tight, ready to smack down on the hard ground.

"Huh?"

Something soft broke my fall.

"Gotcha, Jackie."

Wilson caught me in his arms.

He held me like a baby. Great. Just great . . .

I heard clapping. Mia clapping.

Then Wilson dropped me on the pavement.

"Owwww!" My head hit the cement with a thud.

"Are you okay?" Mia's voice sounded far away.

"Yes, I'm —" I started to answer, struggling to sit up. That's when I saw that Mia wasn't paying any attention to me.

She was bent over Wilson, studying a swollen finger he held out to her.

"I'm okay," Wilson assured her. "Jack doesn't weigh much."

"Nooooo!" Mrs. Green shrieked. "Olive — nooooo!"

Olive dangled from the tree limb by one little paw!

Wilson scrambled up the tree and crawled across the limb. The tree groaned and creaked under his stocky legs. But Wilson didn't care.

He looked so sure of himself as he crossed the sagging branch. He scooped up Olive in one hand. Then he shimmied down the tree trunk.

"Thank you! Thank you!" Mrs. Green threw her arms around Wilson's wide shoulders and hugged him.

My narrow shoulders drooped. I felt miserable.

With Olive cradled safely in her arms, Mrs. Green returned to her house.

I watched her walk across her lawn. My gaze shifted to my yard — where Morty and Terminator wrestled in the grass. Terminator batted Morty with his huge paw. He sent Morty into orbit over the hedges.

Terminator charged across the lawn, jumped over the shrubs, and reached Morty before my poor dog landed. Terminator knocked him out of the air and pounced on him.

Morty yelped helplessly as Terminator pinned him to the ground.

"Terminator, stop!" I shouted, heading over to them.

"Leave them alone. They're just playing!" Wilson called.

But I trudged across the lawn to rescue Morty.

"Even Wilson's dog wins all the time," I grumbled. "Morty and I are losers. Total losers."

"Hey, guys, I've got to go home!" Mia jumped on her bike. "Don't forget about my birthday party on Saturday!"

"I'll be there!" Wilson told her. "And I'm going to bring Terminator. He has a surprise for you."

I groaned.

"Are you coming to my party, Jack?" Mia smiled brightly at me.

"Well — maybe . . ." I tried to come up with a fast excuse.

I *hate* parties.

Don't get me wrong. I like to see my friends — but not at parties. I never really have fun at them — especially if there are party games. I hate to play party games. Especially if Wilson is there.

"I . . . uh . . . may have to go somewhere with my parents," I lied. "I think I promised I'd go with them. And then I promised my dad I'd help clean out the basement."

"You did that last week," Wilson declared. "Remember — I had to help you drag out the trash can. It was too heavy for you."

"Well, we didn't finish," I said, thinking quickly. I'm such a terrible liar.

Mia grasped the gold heart around her neck. "You have to come, Jack. The party doesn't start till six. I really want you to come."

"Well . . . I'll try," I told her.

"Great, Jack. See you!" Mia hopped on her bike and pedaled up the hill toward her house.

Should I go? I asked myself, heading up my driveway.

Mia said she really wants me to come.

So should I forget how much I hate parties — and go?

Yes, I decided.

Yes. Maybe I'll actually have fun.

Yes!

So . . . on Saturday night, I went to Mia's party.

And wouldn't you know it — it ruined my life forever!

4

Mia's house is two blocks up the hill from mine. Her house juts out on stilts. It's kind of dangerous — especially when we have mud slides. But she has an amazing view of the ocean down below.

I stepped up to Mia's front door. I felt really nervous.

For one thing, I'd never met Mia's new stepmother. Mia spends half the year with her real mother in Brentwood. And the other half here in Malibu with her dad and new stepmother.

"Come on in! It's so nice to meet you. I'm Angela Montez," Mia's stepmother greeted me at the door. "Everyone's been waiting for you!"

"Really?" I asked. "For *me*?"

"Really!" Mrs. Montez exclaimed.

Mia's stepmom had the most beautiful smile. I liked her right away.

I followed her to the rec room doorway. She

waved to Mia across the room. "Mia — look who's finally here," she called. "Wilson!"

"Angela — that's not Wilson. That's Jack!" Mia called back.

"Oh. Sorry, Jack." Mrs. Montez patted me on the shoulder. "Well, have a nice time anyway."

Mia grabbed my arm and tugged me forward. The room was jammed with kids. We pushed our way through the crowd.

Red streamers hung from the ceiling. Red is Mia's favorite color. I spotted my friends Ray and Ethan in the crowd. They were opening plastic bags filled with red balloons.

"Hey — Jack. Help us blow these things up," Ray called.

"Okay. Be right there." I liked Ethan and Ray. They were great guys. Fun to hang out with.

I handed Mia her birthday present. I wanted to give her something she would really, really like. I had walked around the mall for hours searching for just the right thing.

"Thanks, Jack. I can't wait to open it!" Mia said, gazing at the red stars on the wrapping paper. "Look! The paper matches my outfit!" Mia pointed to the red stars on her white T-shirt and leggings.

Mia liked the wrapping paper. That made me feel pretty good.

Ray and Ethan tossed over some balloons — the long kind — and we started blowing them up.

After we blew up about fifty of them, we batted them through the air. One after another. Real fast. A storm of red balloons whirled over our heads.

The kids went wild. Leaping up. Batting them back.

"Over here, Jack!" they screamed. "Hit some over here!"

It was cool.

Then Wilson walked in.

"Hey, everyone. Watch this!" He snatched two balloons in flight. He twisted them so fast, his hands moved in a blur. "Ta-da!" He held his creation over his head for everyone to see.

It was the figure of a man — with huge ears, stubby legs, and a fat belly. It looked exactly like our gym teacher, Mr. Grossman.

"Hey! It's The Gross Man!" one of the kids yelled out.

Everyone laughed.

"Awesome, Wilson!" Mia's friend Kara shouted.

"Isn't Wilson a riot?" Mia said to me. "He can do *anything*."

"Yeah," I said, slinking back into the corner of the room. "He's a real riot."

"Make something else!" Mia clapped.

Wilson grabbed some balloons and made a pig with antlers.

And a tiny elephant with a four-foot trunk.

And an enormous chicken.

17

Everyone went crazy over that chicken.

I was almost glad when Mia announced it was time to play Twister. Almost.

I hate Twister. I told you — I hate all party games.

Everyone cleared the center of the room so Mia could set the game out.

I shrank farther back into my corner. I eased myself down to the floor. I did it slowly so no one would notice me.

"Jackie!" Wilson dove over the playing mat and yanked me up. "It's time to see if you can beat the champ!"

Wilson is great at Twister. Of course.

"Uh, Wilson. I don't really feel like playing." I wrestled free of his grip. "I'll spin the spinner so everyone else can play."

"Not necessary, Jack." Wilson's mouth spread into the widest grin I'd ever seen.

I knew that grin meant trouble.

He placed his fingers in his mouth and let out a shrill whistle. Terminator bounded into the room.

"Spin, boy!" Wilson ordered the dog.

Terminator trotted over to the spinner on the floor. He gave it a hard nudge with his nose — and it spun.

Everyone cheered.

"Let's see him *read* it!" I mumbled under my breath.

Mia heard me. "Wilson will probably teach him that next week!" She laughed.

"Right hand red!" someone called out.

Everyone dove for the mat.

Wilson got there first. Of course.

Terminator spun.

"Left foot blue." Mia announced the next move.

Only two moves and we were all a tangled mess. Wilson's position was secure. He's fast. He always finds the easiest spot to land on first.

I'm not that fast.

I had to stretch my left leg way back — over Ray's head — to reach a blue dot.

I felt a sharp pain in my side.

Please, don't let me fall, I prayed. *I don't want to be the first one out. If I am — Wilson will never let me forget it.*

My palms began to sweat.

Three kids had their legs draped over my right arm. I felt my hand slipping off the red dot.

My elbow sagged.

I tried to stiffen it, but it wouldn't stay. It slowly sagged some more.

Wilson craned his neck to see me. "Jack's elbow is touching!" he yelled.

"No, it isn't!" Ethan came to my defense. "Spin, Terminator!"

Terminator spun.

Right foot yellow.

Yellow. Yellow. I searched frantically for a yellow circle. I spotted one.

I hoisted my leg up and over Ray's back.

And that's when I heard the *riiiip*.

My shorts split wide open.

I froze.

"Superman boxers underneath! Cooool!" Wilson hooted.

Everyone laughed.

I glanced over at Mia. She had her head tossed back, laughing like a maniac.

My face burned red.

I jumped up from the game — and staggered from the room.

"Wait, Jack!" Mia chased after me. "Don't go!"

No way I was going to stay.

No way.

I felt totally humiliated.

Mia caught up to me and blocked the door. "Please?" she asked softly. "Please stay?"

Could I say no?

Of course not.

Mrs. Montez gave me a pair of Mia's brother's shorts to wear, and I returned to the rec room.

Everyone was seated at a long table, eating hot dogs. I had to take the only chair left — next to Wilson.

I lifted up my hot dog. I opened my mouth to take a bite.

"Whoa. Wait a minute!" Wilson pushed my

hand away from my mouth. "You call *that* a hot dog?"

He held his hot dog next to mine. He had a foot-long hot dog. TWICE as big as my regular one.

He threw back his head and howled. Then he gulped down his hot dog in two bites.

He grinned that big, horrible, Wilson grin.

He was driving me CRAZY.

A gross glob of mustard stuck to the corner of his mouth. I wanted to wipe it across his face.

Should I do it? I asked myself. Should I give him a mustard bath?

Before I could move, Mia announced it was time to open the presents. Wilson jumped up and headed into the living room — where the presents sat, piled high. Everyone followed.

Mia opened Kara's present first — a bunch of hair scrunchies with red hearts. Then she opened Ray and Ethan's present. A butterfly jigsaw puzzle — with over a thousand pieces.

Mia reached for my present next.

I held my breath.

She carefully untied the red ribbon. Then she ripped the paper open — and gasped.

"Ohhh, Jack!" she exclaimed. "How did you know I wanted this one?" She held up my present for everyone to see. "It's the new CD from my favorite group — Purple Rose."

I knew she would love it.

"Thank you, Jack!" She set my present down

on a table beside her. She reached for the next one. An envelope — just an envelope. No gift.

"That's mine," Wilson leaned over and whispered to me.

I can't believe Wilson only brought Mia a card, I thought as I watched her tear open the flap. Only a card for her birthday. What kind of present is that?

Mia stared into the envelope for a moment. Then she screamed. "Oh, wow! Oh, wow! Oh, wow!"

She held up Wilson's present.

Two tickets.

Two tickets to the Purple Rose concert at the Hollywood Bowl next month.

Front row seats.

"Oh, wow!" she shrieked again. "This is totally awesome!"

Wilson shot me his big Wilson grin.

I couldn't take it any longer. I let out a furious scream — and ran out of the house.

5

I ran down the path from Mia's house as fast as I could.

Ran down the dark road. A single street lamp cast a weak glow over the houses. Trees and shrubs poked over the path as if reaching for me.

I didn't know where I was going — and I didn't care. I just had to get away from the party.

"Stop, Jack! Come back!" I heard Mia call.

I glanced back and saw Mia charging after me. Ray, Ethan, and Kara were chasing me too.

I didn't slow down. I followed the winding path down the hill. I ran right past my house and kept on running.

"Jack! Come back!" Mia shouted.

I shot another glance over my shoulder. They were catching up.

I ran harder. Past some darkened houses that were set back in the hill, hidden behind trees.

I picked up speed as the road continued to

curve downward. Practically flying down now. My toes jammed against the front of my sneakers as I ran. I couldn't stop if I wanted to.

I ran until the road leveled out at the bottom of the hill — where a fence stretched out for miles, separating the beach from the road.

I darted across the road and charged through the fence.

"Jack! Jack!" My friends' voices drifted down the hillside, over the steady roar of the ocean in front of me.

I peered up and down the stretch of beach. Staring at house after house. They sprawled out on the high part of the beachfront, with steps that led down to the sand. Lights from the houses washed over the sand, making the beach bright and silvery.

No place to hide.

No place . . .

Suddenly, an idea flashed into my mind.

The abandoned Dorsey house. I could hide there. The Dorsey house used to be one of the most beautiful beach houses in Malibu. But no one had lived in it in years. Just a big, old wreck now. A great place to hide!

"Jack! Where are you?" Mia's voice floated over the fence.

Better hurry. Before they catch up.

I ran down the beach, past houses with swim-

ming pools and tennis courts. I ran and ran —
and finally, I came to the Dorsey house.

I stopped and stared at it. What a wreck!

The wide, two-story house once had a long
awning that stretched all along the deck. But the
awning had fallen from its poles. The torn canvas
lay heaped on the deck, flapping in the ocean
breeze.

I stepped carefully. Several boards were miss-
ing from the deck. Others were cracked and broken.

I leaped over a hole and made my way to the
door. I turned the knob.

The wooden door had swollen from the con-
stant wetness. I had to ram my shoulder against
it to get it to open. I ducked inside.

"Jack! Where are you?" Ray's voice rang out
from the side of the house.

I quietly closed the door behind me.

An aroma of rotting wood and sour mold
greeted me. I squinted in the darkness, trying to
figure out what room I was in.

I stood in an entranceway. Beyond it, in front
of me, was a living room. Two chairs with ripped
seat cushions stood against one wall. The back
wall of the room was completely made of glass.
Outside I could see the dark ocean waves crash-
ing against the shore.

To the left was a kitchen. To the right, a long

hall. That's where the bedrooms probably are, I thought, as I made my way slowly toward them, leaning one hand on the damp wall.

"Jaaack. Jaaack." My friends' shouts drifted through the closed windows. But they were fading now. Distant.

I walked into a bedroom. Empty — except for a bare mattress on the floor that the Dorseys had left behind.

Back in the hall, I groped the walls. Trying to find my way in the dark.

I stumbled forward — and tripped. Over something big. It landed on the floor with a loud *CRASH*!

I jumped back in fear. Then leaned over to see what it was. Just an old surfboard, I realized. I let out a long sigh.

I moved back into the entranceway. Into the kitchen. The wooden floor creaked beneath my feet.

A shaft of moonlight filtered in through the grimy windows. Some broken mugs lay on one of the counters. A child's sand pail and shovel rested in a corner on the floor.

I stood in the shaft of moonlight.

I could hear the ocean waves pound against the shore.

The wind began to howl outside. It whipped through the weathered boards of the old house. The wood creaked and groaned.

I peered out the kitchen window and saw the clump of fallen awning shivering in the wind, like a ghost getting ready to rise.

Something scampered across my feet.

I let out a startled cry.

A mouse? A rat?

Something bigger?

My entire body shuddered.

This place was really creepy at night.

It's safe to leave now, I told myself. No more voices. They're gone. They're probably all back at Mia's — eating birthday cake.

I bet Wilson is on his third piece, I thought with disgust.

I couldn't wait to get home — to my nice, dry house.

I walked slowly through the darkened kitchen, across the sagging floor. The planks groaned with each step I took.

The door came into view.

I was almost there. Almost out of this cold, creepy house.

I took another step — and the floor broke away.

The wooden planks crashed someplace below — as I plunged down into the gaping hole.

My hands grabbed onto a jagged piece of floorboard. My legs dangled beneath me.

"Help!" I screamed.

But no one could hear me.

I tried to pull myself up. Up out of the hole.

The wooden planks under my hands creaked as I struggled to hoist myself up.

And then the planks splintered. And broke.

I dropped through the hole fast.

Down. Straight down.

6

Into an underground pit?

No.

Into the basement.

I landed hard on my hands and knees.

Pain shot through my body. Then quickly faded.

Luckily, the floor was soft and spongy from all the dampness, so I wasn't really hurt.

I took a deep breath — and choked on the bitter smell of mildew. Yuck! I could even taste it on my tongue.

This was all Wilson's fault!

Wilson — always proving that he's the best.

Never giving me a break.

Okay, okay. Forget about Wilson, I told myself. Calm down. You have to find a way out of this disgusting basement.

I stood up and searched for stairs, a door, a window. But I couldn't see a thing. Too dark. As if a heavy black blanket had been thrown over everything.

My sneakers sank into the decaying floor as I made my way blindly through the room.

My knee bumped into something. A chair?

I reached down and ran my hands over it. Yes, a chair.

Good. If there's a chair down here, maybe I can stand on it. Climb back up into the kitchen. Or climb out a basement window.

I moved slowly through the room. I sloshed through a deep puddle. The cold water seeped through my sneakers.

I'm going to get you for this, Wilson.

I tripped over a table — and something crashed to the floor. I heard glass shatter.

And then I heard a splash.

My heart skipped a beat.

Another animal? Another mouse or rat?

I didn't want to think about it. My temples began to pound.

How was I going to get out of here?

Should I scream for help?

Who would hear me down here? No one — that's who.

On trembling legs, I moved through the room. Hands out in front of me. Groping in the dark.

I stumbled into another table. I ran my hands over it. No — not a table. More like a bench. A workbench. My hands brushed across its top. I felt a hammer, a screwdriver, and — a candle!

My fingers scrambled over the workbench, searching for a match to light it. I groped my way across the entire workbench.

No matches.

I backed away from the bench — and my sneaker rolled over something round. Something round — like a flashlight!

I picked it up. Yes! A flashlight!

My fingers shook as I fumbled for the switch. *Please work. Please work. Please work.*

I flicked it on.

A pale yellow beam of light reached weakly into the gloom.

The flashlight was dim — but I could see!

"I'm out of here!" I cheered.

I swept the weak beam of light in front of me. I had fallen into a small room. Thick cobwebs draped the peeling walls.

A rusty washing machine and clothes dryer sat in one corner. A small, wooden table and a smashed lamp lay on the floor in front of them.

I moved the light closer — and saw a battered camp trunk. I ran my hand over the lid. Yuck. It was covered with a thick layer of damp, smelly mold.

The trunk's rusted hinges creaked as I lifted the top. I pointed my flashlight beam inside. Nothing in there. Nothing but an old book.

I read the title out loud — *"Flying Lessons."*

I flipped through the yellowed pages, searching for pictures of airplanes. I love airplanes. But there wasn't a single plane inside.

The pages were filled with old-fashioned drawings — of humans flying through the air.

People of all ages — men with white beards, women in long dresses, children in funny, old clothing — all soaring through the sky.

What a strange, old book.

I flipped through more pages — until I heard another splash.

I swept my flashlight over the floor — and gasped.

"Ohhhhh. Nooooo." A low wail escaped my lips.

I moved the pale light back and forth, hoping I wasn't seeing what I was seeing.

But even in the dim light, I could see the dark bodies, the tiny eyes glowing red, the open-toothed jaws.

Rats!

Dozens of rats. Scuttling across the floor. Moving in on me.

I leaped back.

I gaped in horror as they closed in.

Sharp toenails clicked against the floor. Scraggly tails swished through the filthy puddles as they scurried forward.

A gray sea of rats.

I froze in terror. I gripped the flashlight tightly to stop it from shaking.

The rats snapped their jaws. They began to hiss. The ugly sound echoed off the damp walls of the small room.

Dozens of tiny red eyes glowed up at me.

The hissing grew louder. Louder. Jaws snapped. Tails swished back and forth. The creatures scuttled over one another, eager to get to me.

And then a big fat rat darted out to the front of the pack. It glared up at me hungrily with glowing red eyes. It bared sharp fangs.

I tried to back away. But I hit the wall.

Nowhere to run.

The rat uttered a shrill cry. It pulled back on its hind legs — and sprang forward.

7

"Noooo!" I screamed and tried to dodge away.

The rat clawed at the bottom of my shorts.

It held on for a second, gnashing its teeth. Then it lost its hold and slid to the floor with a wet *plop*.

Another rat leaped to attack.

I thrashed my leg wildly — and kicked the rat across the room.

Red eyes glowed up at me. The hissing grew to a shrill siren.

I batted rats away with the old book. I swept my flashlight across the room, frantically searching for a way out.

There! A narrow staircase across the room!

I ran for it. Stepping into the sea of rats. Stomping hard on them — flattening their scraggly tails.

Claws scraped against my bare legs as I ran. Two rats clung to my sneakers as I charged up the stairs.

I kicked the rats off. Heard their bodies thumping wetly onto the floor.

Then I staggered the rest of the way up. Hurtled to the door. And out. Out into the fresh air. Gasping. My heart pounding. Sucking in breath after breath of the salty, ocean air.

I ran all the way home. I didn't stop until I came to my house. Panting hard, I collapsed on the front lawn.

I stared into the living-room window. The lamps glowed through the sheer white drapes. I could see Mom and Dad inside.

I started to go in — when I realized that I still clutched the book.

Uh-oh. I knew that Mom and Dad would be upset if they knew I took something that didn't belong to me. Worse than that, they'd start asking me a thousand questions:

Where did you get the book?

What were you doing in that abandoned house?

Why weren't you at the party?

I can't let them see it, I decided.

My wet sneakers squeaked across the lawn as I made my way around back to the garage.

I stepped carefully inside. We have the most cluttered garage in town. My dad likes to collect things. Lots of things. We can't get our car inside the garage anymore. We can't even close the door.

I made my way around a dentist's spit-sink and

the aluminum steps to Mrs. Green's old swimming pool. I hid the book inside a torn mattress, then went into the house.

"Jack, is that you?" Mom called from the kitchen.

"Uh-huh," I answered, jogging upstairs before she saw me. I didn't want to explain my wet, muddy shorts. Shorts that weren't even mine!

"How was the party?" Mom called.

"Um. Okay," I called back. "I left a little early."

"We'll be back tonight, Jack." Dad met me on the front lawn. It was the next morning, and Mom and Dad were getting ready to leave on an all-day trip.

Dad patted me on the shoulder. "This is going to be our lucky trip. The BIG one. The really BIG one. I can feel it."

Dad is always saying that. He's a talent agent. But he doesn't have any really big acts. Nobody famous. Just a few actors with small parts. One plays a train conductor on a TV show. Every week he has the same line. "All aboard." That's it. "All aboard." Week after week.

And he is Dad's most famous client.

So Dad spends most of his time searching for the BIG one. The act that will become famous and make Dad a lot of money.

Today Mom and Dad were driving to Anaheim to listen to a new musical group.

"I hope they aren't crazy," I said to Dad. Last week a real nut auditioned for Dad. She played a Beethoven symphony by banging on her head. After two notes, she knocked herself out — and Dad had to take her to the hospital.

"No. This group sent me a tape." Dad's eyes lit up. "And they sound really great."

Mom hurried out of the house and headed toward the car. "Come on, Ted," she called to Dad. "We don't want to be late. I left dinner in the fridge for you, Jack. See you later!"

Morty and I watched Mom and Dad drive off. We played catch with a Frisbee — until the phone rang.

It was Mia.

"I — I'm sorry I ruined your party," I stammered.

"No problem," she replied cheerfully. "You didn't ruin my party at all. We all went back inside and had a great time."

"Oh. Okay. So — what are you doing today?" I asked. "Want to go Rollerblading?"

I love Rollerblading. I can speed around sharp turns on one foot. And I skate faster than everyone in the whole neighborhood — including Wilson.

"Sure! That's why I called!" she exclaimed. "Wilson got these new blades. With balls underneath instead of wheels. They're much faster than the regular kind."

"Oh. I just remembered. I can't go skating," I told her. "I have to stay home and — water the plants."

Mia hung up.

I peeked out through the living room window. I watched Wilson's house across the street. Waited for Wilson to leave — with his new, stupid in-line skates.

A few seconds later, he sped down his driveway and rolled down the block in a blur.

I let out a long sigh and shuffled outside.

"Come on, Morty!" I snatched the Frisbee from the lawn. "Catch, boy!"

I tossed the Frisbee.

Morty let it soar over his head.

He didn't budge.

Great. Now what?

"Hey! Morty — I know. Let's go find that big book I brought home."

Morty followed me to the garage. I slipped my hands into the lumpy mattress and pulled it out. I lugged the book into the kitchen.

I started to read it — and gasped in amazement.

"Morty — I don't believe this!"

"Wow! Morty! I can fly!"

Morty cocked his furry head at me.

"I know it sounds weird, boy. But it says so right here!" I pointed to the page I was reading. "Humans can fly!"

Wait a minute. Am I crazy? Have I totally lost it? People cannot fly.

Morty jumped up on a kitchen chair. He stared down at the book. At a picture of a young girl. With arms stretched out to her sides, she sailed through the air — her long, blond hair flowing behind her.

Morty glanced up at me. Peered back down at the page. Then he whimpered and bolted from the room.

"Come back, Morty. Don't you want to learn to fly?" I laughed. "Morty — The First and Only Flying Dog!"

I turned back to the book and read:

"For as long as humans have walked the earth,

39

they have yearned to fly. To float like an angel. To glide like a bat. To soar like a mighty bird of prey.

"All a dream. A hopeless dream — until now.

"The ancient secret of human flight is a simple one.

"You need only three things: the daring to try, an imagination that soars, and a good mixing bowl."

Hey —! I stared at the page. I had those things. Maybe I should give it a try. I had nothing better to do today.

I read on.

There, on the next page, the book told *exactly* what you needed to do to fly.

It gave some exercises to practice. And a magical mixture you had to eat.

Learn the Motion, Eat the Potion — that's what it said.

Finally it gave an ancient chant to recite.

And that was it. The secret of flying — right there.

Yeah, right. I rolled my eyes.

I scanned the list of ingredients I would need to make the potion. The main ingredient was yeast — "because yeast rises."

Hmmm. Yeast *does* rise. Maybe this really would work. Maybe I really could learn to fly.

If I could — it would be awesome. I would soar through the sky — just like my superheroes.

I could fly, I thought dreamily as I searched

the pantry for the yeast. *Something Wilson couldn't do in a million years!*

And, boy, would Mia be impressed.

I could hear her now. "Oh, wow! Oh, wow! Oh, wow!" she would scream as I flew into the sky, leaving Wilson down on the ground — like a bug.

I'm going to do it right now! I'm going to learn how to fly!

Of course I knew it was crazy. But what if it worked? What if it really worked?

I turned to the page with the exercises. "Step One," I read out loud. "Hold your arms straight out in front of you. Bend your knees slightly. Now take fifty little hops in this position."

I did it. I felt like an idiot, but I did it.

"Step Two. Sit on the floor. Place your left foot on your right shoulder. Then lift your right leg and tuck it behind your head."

This was harder to do. A lot harder. I tugged my left foot up until it reached my shoulder. A sharp pain shot down my side. But I wasn't giving up.

I lifted my right leg up, up, up to my chin — then I lost my balance and rolled onto my back!

I tried it again. This time I rolled to the side.

Learning to fly wasn't going to be as easy as I thought.

I tried one more time — and got it.

But now I was stuck — all twisted up. My left foot perched on my right shoulder, with my toes jammed in my ears. My other foot pressed against the back of my head — shoving my face into my chest.

I struggled to untangle myself.

I stopped struggling when I heard someone laugh.

And realized I wasn't alone.

"What . . . are . . . you . . . doing?"

"Ray, is that you?" I tried to look up, but I couldn't. My chin was slammed tight against my chest.

"Yes, it's me. Ethan is here, too. *What* are you doing?" he repeated.

"He must be practicing for Twister," Ethan suggested.

They both laughed.

"Very funny, guys," I said. "Can you pull me apart? I think I'm stuck."

Ray and Ethan untangled me. "Whoa, that feels better," I said, stretching out my arms and legs.

"So — what *were* you doing?" Ethan asked the question this time.

"Exercising," I mumbled. "I was exercising. To . . . uh . . . improve my tennis game."

"Whoa. Those were pretty weird exercises." Ethan's eyebrows arched way up.

"He wasn't exercising for tennis!" Ray exclaimed. "He doesn't even play tennis!"

"I'm thinking of taking it up," I said quickly.

Ray narrowed his eyes at me. He didn't believe me. But he didn't ask any more questions.

"Want to shoot some hoops in the playground?" Ethan asked.

I didn't want to go anywhere.

I wanted to stay home. Alone. And see if I could fly.

"No, I have to stay home with Morty," I lied. "He's not feeling well."

Morty heard his name and charged full speed into the kitchen. He leaped on Ray and licked his face.

"He looks okay to me," Ray said, narrowing his eyes at me again.

"No problem. We can stay here," Ethan suggested. "Toss a football around or something."

Ethan glanced around the kitchen. His eyes fell on the book.

"No. Sorry. I really can't hang out," I said, tossing the book in the trash can. "I have to clean up the kitchen." I turned to the counter and wiped it with a sponge. Then I began lining up the spices in the spice rack — labels facing out.

"And I have to stay inside anyway. To wait for Mom and Dad to call. They're away. They said to sit by the phone."

"Why?" Ethan asked. "What's so important?"

"They wouldn't tell me. They said it's a surprise." I shrugged my shoulders.

"Okay, see you later — maybe," Ray said. Both guys were shaking their heads as they left.

I grabbed the book out of the garbage and flipped back to the exercise page.

I read the flapping and leaping exercises next. I did them all.

Now it was time to say the magic words.

I read them to myself first. To make sure I got them right. Then I recited them out loud, slowly.

Hishram hishmar shah shahrom shom.

I climbed up on the kitchen chair — and jumped off. To see if I felt different. Lighter. Floaty.

I landed with a hard *thud*.

Guess I need to eat the special flying food for the full effect, I decided. I turned back to the book.

It was time to start mixing.

In a cabinet next to the refrigerator, I found our good mixing bowl. I dumped all the ingredients into it: 10 egg yolks, 1 tablespoon of maple syrup, 2 cups of flour, 1/2 cup of seltzer, and 4 tablespoons of yeast.

I stirred. A lumpy yellow blob of dough started to form.

I turned the page to read the next step.

"You are about to embark on the most glorious

adventure in the history of time," I read out loud. "You alone will fly with the falcons. You alone will sail toward the sun. Are you ready?"

I nodded yes.

"You say, yes?"

I nodded yes again.

"You are wrong. You are not ready. Turn the page."

I turned the page — to the last page in the book.

"Empty one quarter of contents of envelope into bowl. Mix well."

Envelope! What envelope?

The rest of the page was blank — except for a tiny spot of dried glue.

I ran my finger over the glue spot. That's where the envelope had been.

But where was it now?

I shook the book frantically.

Nothing fell out.

"Oh, no," I groaned. "No envelope . . . no envelope . . ."

Wait! I know!

I ran over to the trash can.

There it was!

A small black envelope. It must have fallen out when I tossed the book into the trash.

I opened it up. Measured one quarter of the bright blue powder inside — and dropped it into the bowl.

I mixed well.

The yellow blob of dough turned green. Then it began to grow and bubble. Small bubbles at first — popping lightly on the surface. Then larger ones — growing from deep inside the dough. Rising to the surface. Bursting open with a loud *PLOP*.

PLOP. PLOP. PLOP.

Yuck!

I stood back.

The dough began to throb — like a beating heart.

I watched in horror as it started to gurgle.

I gulped.

What was in that envelope? Maybe it was some kind of poison!

Forget about flying. No way am I eating this gross garbage! I decided.

No way.

10

I grabbed the sides of the bowl — to dump the mixture into the trash. But I snatched my hands back when the dough flopped over, all by itself.

It flopped again and again, each time making a sickening sucking sound.

My stomach lurched.

I reached out again — and the phone rang.

"We're on our way home, Jack." Dad was calling from the car. He sounded disappointed.

"So soon?" I asked. "What happened?"

"The band members had a big fight. They called us in the car. They said don't bother coming to Anaheim. They broke up the act." I heard Dad sigh.

"Wow, Dad. I don't know what to say."

"Not to worry, Jack. I still feel lucky. Don't know why. But I do. The BIG one is coming. I can feel it. We're on the freeway. Should be home in half an hour," he said. Then he hung up.

Ugh. I better dump this stuff before they get back, I told myself.

I turned to the kitchen table — and shrieked in horror. "Morty — no! NO! What have you done?"

11

"Morty! DOWN!" I screamed.

Morty stood on the kitchen chair.

His front paws rested on the table.

His head dipped into the mixing bowl — as he swallowed a big glob of green dough.

"NO, Morty! DOWN!" I screamed again.

Morty lifted his head.

He licked his chops.

Then dove into the bowl for another bite.

I sprang across the room.

I peered down into the bowl.

"Oh, noooo!" I howled. Almost half the dough was gone!

"Morty! What did you do!" I pulled his head out of the bowl.

Morty stared up at me — his eyes wide with guilt. His ears drooped low.

He whimpered softly. Then he dipped his head back into the bowl for another bite.

I scooped him off the chair.

Carried him into the living room — and gasped as he floated up out of my hands.

I stared in disbelief as Morty floated through the room. Back into the kitchen.

"Morty — you're flying!" I cried.

It worked! I couldn't believe it! My cocker spaniel was FLYING!

I followed him — in a daze.

Followed him as he floated over the kitchen table.

Watched in amazement as he flew out the open window.

"Morty!" I cried, jolted back to reality. "Wait!"

Morty let out a sharp yelp — then sailed up, up into the sky.

I ran outside — and gazed up.

Morty soared above the house.

Floating higher and higher.

"Morty — no! Morty!" I screamed. "Morty — come back!"

His legs thrashed as he floated over the treetops. He started barking, shrill, sharp yelps of terror.

"Morty —! Morty —!"

I watched him sail up, his body rocked by the wind, his legs scrambling as if trying to grab hold of something.

"Oh, nooooo!" I wailed, staring helplessly.

I've got to get him back! I've got to rescue Morty!

But how?

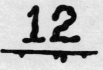

12

I knew how.

I knew how to rescue my dog. And I knew I had no choice.

I ran in to the house.

I plunged my hand into the bowl. Grabbed up a big chunk of the disgusting mixture.

Yuck! I can't eat this! IT FEELS SO SLIMY!

You have to eat it, I ordered myself. You have to save Morty. It's the only way!

The dough throbbed and gurgled in my palm.

A thin mist of steam rose up from my fingers.

"Ohhh," I groaned as I shoved a fistful of the stuff into my mouth.

I clutched my throat. I started to gag.

It tasted sour and hot. It scorched my tongue.

I choked it down.

And grabbed up another glob.

Shoved it into my mouth. Swallowed hard.

My mouth and tongue swelled. Swelled with the horrible, bitter taste.

I shoved in another handful. I had to make sure I could fly like Morty.

I could feel the mixture throbbing as it slid down my throat.

Gagging, I ran back outside.

I gazed up into the sky.

Morty flew high over the trees. His cries drifted down to the ground.

I could see his legs still flailing wildly as he floated higher and higher.

He looked so small up there.

Just a dark speck in the sky now.

"I'm coming, Morty!" I cupped my hands around my mouth and yelled. "Don't worry, boy. I'll save you!"

I raised my arms up to the sky.

"I WILL FLY!" I cried out. "FLY!"

I took a strong leap.

Nothing happened.

13

Speed.

That's it.

I need to build up speed.

I ran around my backyard. I circled it three times.

Faster and faster.

My sneakers ripped the grass. I ran hard, as hard as I could.

Sweat poured down my face.

I'm ready. I'm definitely ready now, I thought, gasping for air.

I raised my arms over my head.

I leaped high.

And came down.

Nothing.

"I don't get it!" I wailed. "Why can't I —"

I know! The exercises!

The hopping exercises. That must be it!

I stretched my arms straight in front of me.

Then I took off — hopping around the backyard on both feet at super warp speed.

HOP. HOP. HOP.

HOP. HOP. HOP.

I hopped around the backyard like a crazed bunny.

This is it. I'm ready. I know it, I thought, hopping frantically.

"Morty! I'm coming!"

Still hopping, I bent my knees to lower myself.

Still hopping, I lifted my arms up over my head.

Then, with one mighty hop, I launched myself off the ground.

And came back down.

"What's wrong?" I struggled to breathe. "Why can't I fly like Morty?"

Morty!

I gazed up. Morty drifted in front of a cloud — a tiny black speck now.

"Oooh, Morty! Come back!" I cried — and a horrible taste flooded my mouth. The bitter taste of the dough.

I could feel it throbbing in my stomach. Churning.

I could hear it gurgling in there.

Bubbling up. Up through my chest. Into my throat. Into my mouth.

I burped —

— and took off!

My feet blasted off the ground — and I shot high into the air.

I was flying!

"I can't believe it! I'm flying. I'm really flying! Like a superhero."

"Whooooa!" I thrashed my arms and legs wildly. I rose up and up — out of control!

I floated over my house.

Over the trees.

Over the hills of Malibu. I could see the blue ocean, sparkling far below.

Morty continued to sail up. Up and away from me.

"Morty, I'm coming!" I shouted.

I kept my eyes locked on Morty. I tried to aim my body in his direction.

"Whooooa!" I did a somersault in the air. I whirled over and over. And stopped — with my head pointed down and my feet sticking up.

The wind pulled me higher. I couldn't flip around. My feet were still straight up. All the blood was rushing down to my head!

I floated higher. Up through a cloud.

I gasped for air. I struggled to turn. Suddenly, I felt faint.

Superheroes don't fly feet first! I scolded myself. *Do something!*

I brought my knees to my chest — and my body spun around.

It worked. I was right-side up.

But now Morty was behind me.

I twisted in the air — struggling to turn, struggling to catch sight of him.

Yes! I could see Morty — floating even higher.

I floated up, up — toward him.

Closer . . . closer.

"Hold on, Morty," I called. "I'm almost there!"

I felt a rush of wind in my face.

Two robins soared past, swooping out of my path.

I peered down. My house and garage looked like toys — so tiny. Wilson's house looked even smaller than mine. Ha!

I was flying! I couldn't believe it! I was really, really flying.

I floated up. Close to Morty. He stared at me, whimpering, his whole body trembling as he floated.

"Hold on, boy." I stretched out my hands. But I couldn't reach him.

I floated closer. I tried to pick up speed, but I didn't know how. All I could do was float on the air currents. Float in the direction they carried me.

I grabbed for the dog again. Missed.

He floated two or three feet from my grasp.

I'm going to lose Morty forever! I thought.

A stiff breeze picked me up.

I shot ahead on it. But so did Morty.

I could hear his terrified whimpers as he floated up toward the blazing sun.

I floated closer . . . closer. I stretched out my hands again. I could almost touch him now. Almost.

It was so hot up here. I felt as if I were burning up. And poor Morty. His little body heaved in the heat.

His head drooped limply. His tongue sagged out.

He wasn't going to make it!

I floated closer. I reached out again . . . and . . . GOT HIM!

I pulled Morty into my arms. His entire body shook. I held him snugly against my chest — and gazed down as I floated higher . . . higher.

HIGHER.

Oh, no!

A terrifying thought suddenly gripped me.

I'm just going to keep floating higher. And higher. I don't know how to get down!

14

I drifted higher.

My temples pounded.

The world beneath me began to shrink — smaller and smaller.

I could barely make out my house now — it looked as if it could fit in the palm of my hand. In the distance, the ocean stretched like a blue carpet. The beach was a slender yellow ribbon.

I felt dizzy. Sick.

Morty gazed down and whimpered.

"It's okay, boy," I told him. "We're going home now."

But how? HOW?

I shifted Morty into one arm. I stretched out my other arm. Pointed it to my right.

I swerved to the right!

Hey — not bad!

I pointed to my left — and flew to the left!

This was great!

I pointed my arm down.

Whoaaa! I started to dive.

I brought my arm up quickly — and soared straight ahead.

If I held my feet tightly together, I picked up speed. When I separated them slightly — I slowed down.

Awesome!

I sailed through the sky. I floated. Glided. Drifted. Soared. I even flew on my back!

I let the breeze gently lift me up. Then I lowered my arm and swooped down, then up again.

I gazed at the hills below. At the houses that nested in them.

The houses seemed to dot the hills in a perfect pattern — right down to the beach front.

I could see Mrs. Green's pool — the size of a postage stamp from up here. A sparkling blue postage stamp.

And the ocean — the ocean! I flew low over the waves, holding Morty tightly, feeling the cold, refreshing spray on my face.

Then I soared back up to the hills. Funny, I thought. Gazing at the world from way up here should seem scary. But it isn't scary at all.

In fact, it feels safer. Calmer. Not as confusing as when you're in it, down below.

I held my feet tightly together and soared over my school.

"Hey! Morty! Look who's on the playground! There's Ray and Ethan! Shooting baskets."

I swooped low behind some treetops, then flew toward home. I didn't want Ray and Ethan to see me. I didn't want to show them that I could fly — not yet.

I wanted to show Mia first. Mia. Wait till she sees this, I thought, soaring higher.

And wait till Wilson sees me fly. HA! This will shut him up — FOREVER!

I floated through the air, dreaming about all the things I would do — now that I could fly.

I gazed down at my house.

And saw our car roll up the driveway. "Oh no, Morty! Mom and Dad are home!"

Did they see me?

If they did, I was doomed.

They would think it was way too dangerous up here.

They would never let me fly.

Please, please — don't let them see me! I prayed.

"Hey — look up there!" I heard Dad cry.

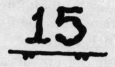

15

I swooped down behind the garage.

I placed Morty gently on the ground.

"What did you see?" I heard Mom ask Dad.

"A bird on the garage roof," Dad replied. "I thought it was a condor."

"They're so rare," Mom commented, slamming the car door.

Whew! I breathed a sigh of relief. They hadn't seen me.

"Hey — !" I gasped when I realized that Morty had started to rise up again. "Down, boy! Down!" I cried. I tied the end of his leash to a small rock.

He took a few wobbly steps. He didn't have any trouble walking with the rock. And it was just the right size to keep him grounded. He headed straight for his doghouse.

I charged into the kitchen.

What a mess.

Powdery trails of yeast and flour stained the kitchen floor. Cracked eggshells sat in a slimy puddle of yolk on the table. And globs of the horrible green dough stuck to the kitchen chairs, the counters — everywhere.

I could hear Mom and Dad unlocking the front door.

No time to clean up.

I tucked the small black envelope into the flying book. And I ran out the back door with the book. I tore out to the garage and slid the book back into the folds of the old mattress.

"Jack! We're home!" Dad shouted through the house.

"Where are yoooou?" I heard Mom call.

"Hi, Mom! Hi, Dad!" I burst through the back door, into the kitchen.

"Whoa! What happened in here?" Dad gazed around the room, wide-eyed.

Mom sniffed the air. "What is that horrible smell?"

"In here?" I stalled, trying to come up with a good excuse.

Mom and Dad nodded, staring at me. Waiting for an explanation.

"Oooh, you mean in here," I said, sweeping an arm through the air. "Uh . . . just a science experiment. For school. It didn't quite work out."

I woke up really early the next morning. I wanted to try to fly again. Before school. Before Mom and Dad woke up.

I dressed quickly. I walked silently into the kitchen.

"Hey, Jack! You're up early!" Dad sat at the kitchen table, eating breakfast. "It's only five A.M.!"

"I — I couldn't sleep," I said, shocked to find him there. "What are *you* doing up?"

"The phone woke me up. It was a guy who said he had an act I *had* to see — 'Nelson and His Amazing Needles.'"

"Amazing Needles." I gulped. "What does this guy do?"

"Well, Nelson is not a guy," Dad started to explain. "Nelson is a chimpanzee. And his needles are knitting needles. His owner says Nelson can knit a sweater in ten minutes. Sleeves and all."

A monkey that knits? I let out a long sigh.

Dad sighed, too.

"Well, the phone call wasn't a total waste. At least I'll get an early start today," Dad said, finishing his breakfast.

By the time he left, Mom was out of bed. Too late to try to fly now.

I'll have to wait till after school. Mom will be at work. Dad won't be home either. That's when I'll fly for Mia, I decided.

I couldn't wait!

When the last bell rang, I charged out of school before Mia and Wilson could catch up.

I didn't talk to them all day. I didn't want to

talk to them now. I was afraid I might give away my secret. Afraid I might tell them that I could fly. And I didn't want to do that.

I wanted to show them!

I ran all the way home. I threw down my backpack. Poured myself a tall glass of orange juice. For strength.

Then I phoned Mia.

No answer. She wasn't home yet.

I'll give her ten more minutes, I thought, heading into my bedroom. Then I'll call again.

I sat down at my desk and started sketching my newest superhero — ME! I drew myself soaring high over the Hollywood Hills. Sailing way above the big HOLLYWOOD sign.

Maybe I should tell Mom and Dad I can fly, I thought as I sketched. That way I won't have to hide. That way I can fly whenever I want.

No. No way! I decided. They'll think it's way too dangerous. They'll probably think I'm weird, that there is something *wrong* with me. And they won't let me do it. I definitely cannot tell them. I have to keep this a secret.

I held my drawing up and studied it. It needed one last thing. Then it would be perfect. A superhero cape. As I sketched in the cape, I thought about Wilson.

Wilson — and the sick look on his face when he realized that our competition was over for all time.

When he realized that he could never win against me again — ever!

When he saw me flying!

I jumped up from my desk and phoned Mia.

Still no answer.

I wandered over to my bedroom window and peered outside.

Hey! There she was! In front of Wilson's house. With Wilson.

Wilson was skating down his driveway on his fancy, new in-line skates. At the end of the driveway, he had set up a small ramp — and he was rolling full-speed straight for it.

He flew up the ramp — and soared into the air. "Yahoo!" he shouted, shooting his fists up as he swooped down for a perfect landing.

Mia applauded.

Ha! You think that's flying, Wilson? I thought. Your days of showing off are over. Watch this!

I opened my window as high as I could.

I marched across my room — through the bedroom doorway and out into the hall.

I inhaled deeply — and took a running start.

I charged through my bedroom.

I leaped out my bedroom window.

I spread my arms wide.

And fell like a rock.

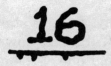

16

"Ooooof!"

I landed on my back in the soft hedges below my window.

The fall knocked the breath out of me. I lay there dazed for about a minute, my chest aching, struggling to breathe.

I moved my arms and legs. They seemed to be okay. Nothing broken.

What went wrong? Can I still fly? I wondered.

Maybe the secret recipe lasts for only one flight.

Or maybe I have to take off from the ground. That could be it. Maybe I'm not supposed to *leap* into flight.

"Jack! Are you okay?" Mia ran over to me. "What happened? Did you *fall* out of the window?"

"Nobody falls out a bedroom window — nobody, but Jack!" Wilson hooted. "How klutzy do you have to be to fall out a window?"

"I did not fall out my bedroom window," I protested. I didn't know what else to say.

"Yes, you did, Jack. We saw you. We saw the whole thing." Wilson snickered. He turned to Mia with a smirk on his face. "Bet Jack was practicing Twister again."

I climbed to my feet. I stared down as I brushed myself off. Stared down so I wouldn't have to look at either one of them.

"Jack, come with me." Wilson tugged my arm. "I want to show you something. Something really important. It could save your life one day. It's called a door."

Mia giggled.

I knocked Wilson's hand away.

I could feel the blood rushing to my face.

Okay, Wilson. That's it! I've had enough of you — you and your bragging and your stupid jokes.

I took a deep breath.

"I want to show *you* both something," I announced.

I placed my feet close together.

I lifted my arms and pointed them in the air.

I hope this works, I prayed. *I hope I don't look like a total jerk.*

I raised myself up on my toes.

Here goes . . .

17

I bent my knees.

I took a deep breath. I shut my eyes.

Prepared to take off . . .

"Jack? Jack? Where *are* you?" a voice called.

"Huh?" I opened my eyes. I lowered my arms slowly.

"Jack?" It was Mom. Home early from work. She poked her head out my bedroom window.

I let out a long sigh. "What is it, Mom?"

"Jack, I meant to catch you before you went out. This spring cleaning is too much for one person. I need some help cleaning Dad's closet. Can you come in and give me a hand?"

"Okay, Mom. Be right there."

Mom ducked back inside. "Jack?" Mom popped her head back out.

"Yeah?"

"Is Morty okay? He hasn't left his doghouse since yesterday."

"Don't worry, Mom. He's okay. He got a lot of exercise yesterday. He's just kind of pooped."

Actually, I *tried* to get Morty to come out of his doghouse this morning. But he wouldn't budge. The poor dog was probably afraid he'd float away again.

Wilson headed back to his house. Mia followed. She turned back to me. "Meet us after you're finished helping your mom," she suggested. "Over at Wilson's."

"Yeah, sure," I said, not really planning to.

"You have to try his skating ramp," Mia said. "He built it himself, and it's really awesome. It really sends you flying through the air."

I watched them cross the street.

Flying through the air — Mia's words repeated in my mind. I shook my head.

I'll show you how to fly through the air, Wilson. Just wait.

18

The next afternoon, I ran all the way home from school. I told Mia and Jack to meet me in front of my house. They thought we were going to Rollerblade.

Ha! I had something much better in mind for today.

Today was the day I was going to show them that I could fly!

I dropped my backpack in the hall and ran outside. I glanced up — at the dark, heavy clouds rolling in over the hills.

By the time Mia and Jack showed up, it started to rain — really hard. A bolt of lightning snaked through the sky.

"We'll have to wait until tomorrow," Mia said.

"I guess," I mumbled as I watched them hurry away.

It rained the next day. And the day after that. And the day after that.

No flying.

No chance to show Wilson what a loser he is.

I sat at the window, staring out at the falling raindrops. Was I *ever* going to get my chance to fly?

On Friday, Mia had to go to the dentist after school.

And on Saturday and Sunday, we couldn't get together. I had to work on my term paper. It was due on Monday — and I hadn't even started it.

I wasn't worried about it. I knew exactly what I was going to write about — the history of comic books in the United States.

It was going to be excellent. I knew it.

I got up early Saturday morning and started working on it right away. I sat at my computer for hours. It took me all day to write. Then, on Sunday, I set out my pens and inks and began to illustrate it.

Superman. Spider-Man. Sub-Mariner. The X-Men. All my favorite superheroes.

As I drew the big *S* on Superman's costume, I thought about flying. About how awesome it felt when I soared on a strong current. Or sailed on a gentle breeze.

I pictured myself zooming up from the ground and streaking over the trees. Then slowing down. Drifting lazily among the clouds. Then blasting off again, into the stratosphere — like Superman.

I pictured myself performing all kinds of fancy feats — spirals, nosedives, back flips in the air. I pictured myself doing all these things — for Mia.

And for Wilson . . .

We handed in our term papers on Monday. A rainy Monday.

No flying today either. I sighed. *Who ever heard of so much rain in California?*

The rest of the week remained gray and stormy. The whole week — a total washout.

On Friday, the teacher handed back our term papers.

Yes!

I got a 97! And she wrote "Good job!" across the top.

"Hey, Wilson. Look — ninety-seven!" I held up my paper for him to see. "Pretty good, huh!"

"That *is* pretty good," Wilson agreed. "But it's not excellent!" Wilson smiled gleefully.

He held up his paper.

It had a big, fat 98 written on it.

And the words, "Excellent job!"

I could feel my cheeks begin to burn. Stay calm, I told myself. It won't rain forever.

I woke up the next morning. I bolted to the window. Pushed the curtains aside. The warm rays of the sun splashed across my face.

All right! I pumped both fists into the air.

I called Wilson and Mia and told them to meet me in the park. Right away.

Mia arrived first. Wilson showed up a few minutes later, waving, excitedly.

"Hey, guys — big news!" He charged over to us. "Guess where *I'm* going on spring break."

"Where?" Mia asked eagerly.

"New York City!" he exclaimed. "My parents are taking me to New . . . York . . . City. Can you believe it?"

"That's great!" Mia cheered. She slapped him a high five.

"Where are *you* going for spring break, Jackie?" Wilson asked.

"Uh . . . nowhere. My parents have to work," I murmured.

"Hey — bad break," Wilson said. But I could tell he didn't mean it. "Of course, my trip is no big deal," he went on. "I've been to New York before. Four times."

"*Four* times!" Mia cried. "Really?"

"Yeah," Wilson replied. "Four times. And the last time I was there, I rode the subway — by myself!"

You're right, Wilson, I thought. *New York City is no big deal. Because no one is going to care about your bragging in a few seconds.*

"Hey, Wilson. Want to race?" I asked. "You can practice running for the subway."

"Not funny, Jackie," Wilson replied. "Anyway, what's the point of a race? You know you can't run as fast as I can."

"Come on," I urged. "Race you to the flagpole and back. I'll beat you this time, Wilson. Really."

"No way you can win." He shrugged. "But — okay."

This was it.

My big moment.

My heart began to pound.

I was going to win the race. And shock them both — because I was going to fly!

Wilson and I stood side by side.

"On your mark. Get set —" Mia announced.

I raised my arms high. Pointed them to the sky. Wilson turned to me, staring at my odd racing position.

"GO!" Mia cried.

I took a running leap — and blasted off the ground. I soared up — up over the grass. Into the air. Up toward the treetops.

Yes! Yes! I was flying!

"WHOOOAAA!" Mia shrieked in amazement as I soared with the wind.

Now for the best part.

I peered down to the ground to see the sick look on Wilson's face.

I peered down — and screamed in surprise.

Below me, I saw Wilson.

He was RIGHT below me.

Inches away from me.

Wilson was flying, too.

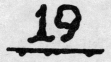

19

"NOOOOO!" I shrieked. "NO WAAAAY!"

I was so shocked — so totally horrified — I dropped my arms to my sides.

Oh, no . . .

I went into a steep dive.

I uttered a weak cry as the ground shot up to meet me — fast.

I kicked my legs. Swung my arms up frantically.

And flew headfirst into a tree trunk.

"Ohhh." Pain shot through my body as I sank to the grass.

Sprawled on my back, I raised my eyes to Wilson. I clutched my stomach, sickened at the sight of him.

Wilson — flying. Wilson — soaring easily to the flagpole and back.

I watched as he gently swooped down. "I win, Jackie!" he exclaimed, making a smooth landing beside me.

"How did you DO THAT!" Mia screamed with excitement.

Wilson planted his hands on his hips. "Aw. It's easy," he bragged. "Nothing to it."

I opened my mouth to speak — but only a tiny squeak came out.

Wilson laughed. "Jackie, you need some propellers or something. Your jets are kind of slow!"

My heart sank.

"How — how —?" I sputtered.

"Oh, I've always known how to fly," Wilson said.

"REALLY?" Mia cried.

"Not really," he laughed. "Jackie taught me how."

"No. No, I didn't!" I managed to choke out.

"Yes, you did, Jack. You just didn't know it!" Wilson hooted. "I saw you flying the day I got my new Rollerblades."

"How did you see him flying?" Mia demanded. "I was with you. How come I didn't see him?"

"Don't you remember?" Wilson replied. "I was skating way ahead of you — because you couldn't keep up with me. So I skated over to Jack's house to show him my new blades — and I saw him fly."

I stood up slowly.

I faced Wilson. Ready to punch out his lights. I admit it. I was out of control.

He had ruined my big moment. Ruined it.

I wanted to punch him like a punching bag. But

somehow I kept myself together. I clenched my fists until they ached.

I had to find out exactly how he learned to fly. "So — you saw me." I narrowed my eyes. "Then what?"

"Then I followed you to your garage. I saw you hide the book in the mattress. And so I . . . *borrowed* it. And I followed the easy instructions."

He grinned at Mia. "I'm like a real superhero." He puffed out his chest. "I love it!"

He turned back to me. "Hey, Jack! You can be my sidekick."

I DON'T WANT TO BE YOUR SIDEKICK, WILSON! I want to win. Just once. Just once, I want to beat you.

That's what I thought — but I didn't say it. I didn't say anything. I just stomped away.

Face it, I told myself glumly as I headed out of the park. You'll never beat Wilson at anything.

"Jack — come back!" Mia called. "I want to see you fly again."

No way, I thought. What was the point now? I kept walking.

"Please, Jack!" Mia cried. "You looked so *awesome* up there. Please do it again!"

I stopped.

Maybe I should fly for Mia. Impress her with some fancy flying maneuvers.

Okay, I decided. I'll fly one more time — to impress her.

I took a deep breath. Then, with my arms stretched out in front of me, I zoomed up. Up to the treetops.

"Go, Jack! Go, Jack! Go, Jack!" Mia chanted, smiling and waving.

I banked to the left and glided through a big fluffy cloud. When I broke through the other side, Wilson was there to meet me.

We flew side by side — looping, diving, then soaring back up. We matched movement for movement — as if we'd practiced together a thousand times.

Then Wilson swooped away from me.

He rolled under me. Jetted behind me. Rolled under me again.

"Yahoo!" I heard him scream from somewhere above me.

I floundered in the air. I didn't know where Wilson was. Where he was going to turn up next.

He circled me — like a mad bird.

"Wilson!" I yelled. "Cut it out!"

"Lighten up, Jackie!" he laughed.

Then, he moved in front of me — blocking my path. Blocking my view.

"Get out of the way!" I screamed. "I'm going to crash into you!"

Wilson let out a roar, like a plane. Then took a steep dive. Now I could see.

Too late.

I smacked hard into a flagpole.

I could hear Wilson's cruel laugh as I tumbled to the ground.

"Excellent landing, Jackie!" he called. He dropped easily to the grass in front of Mia.

Mia clapped and cheered.

"Well, I have to go! I'm late for my tennis game. Want to come?" Wilson asked me.

"I don't play tennis," I replied between clenched teeth.

"Oh. I thought you did," he said, puzzled. "Ray and Ethan told me you were taking lessons. Well, got to go!"

Wilson hurried off.

"Jack — I want to fly too! Please teach me how to fly!" Mia begged.

"I don't know, Mia . . ." I started. "I wanted to keep this kind of secret. I mean — nobody knows about it. Except you and Wilson. If we're *all* flying around Malibu, somebody will find out."

I hated to admit it, but I really didn't want Mia to learn how to fly.

"Jack! You have to show me how. It isn't fair that you and Wilson can fly and I can't!" she wailed. "It isn't fair!"

Whoa. Wait a minute! I told myself. Maybe I *should* teach Mia how to fly. If *I'm* the one to teach her, she'll *really* be impressed. This could be my big chance.

"Okay," I agreed. "I'll teach you how to fly.

Let's go back to my house. We'll get the flying book."

"Thank you! Thank you, Jack!" Mia was so excited, she hugged me.

I led the way to our garage.

"Oooh! I can't wait!" Mia jumped with glee.

I stopped in front of the garage door.

"What are you waiting for, Jack? Open it!" she cried impatiently.

"Weird. It's closed," I said, confused. "The garage door is never closed."

"So — open it!" Mia demanded.

I reached for the handle.

I tugged up the garage door — and cried out in shock.

20

Gone!

Everything — gone. The dentist's spit-sink. Mrs. Green's pool steps. The old mattress. All gone.

I stared at the empty garage in shock.

"Ohhhh, noooo. Dad cleaned out the garage," I moaned unhappily. "Mia — I can't teach you how to fly. The book — is gone."

"You read the book, Jack. You have to remember what it said!" Mia protested. "I want to FLY! Think! You've *got* to remember!"

"It's no use," I told her. "We need the secret ingredient. It was in an envelope. Inside the book. It's gone."

Mia shook her head and uttered an angry groan.

Then a look of calm came over her face. "That's okay, Jack. Maybe it's just as well. This flying thing is kind of scary."

"So — you're not angry at me?" I asked her.

"No," she replied. "It really wasn't your fault. You know what I think, Jack?"

I shook my head. "No. What?"

"I think you shouldn't fly anymore. Or maybe you should tell your parents about it. I mean, it's not normal. I have a very bad feeling about it."

I shrugged.

"Jack — I'm not kidding. I don't think you should fly anymore. It's not safe."

"But I don't want to stop," I protested. "It's so much fun. It's awesome. Totally awesome up there. Besides, what could happen?"

That night after dinner, I hurried to my room to work on a new superhero drawing.

I drew the outline of his figure. I was going to call him Captain Arrow.

I shoved my chair away from my desk. Stared out the window for a while. Returned to my drawing.

I drew a purple leather quiver over Captain Arrow's shoulder — to hold his powerful crimson arrows.

I got up. Looked outside again. I don't know — drawing superheros seemed kind of boring now.

I left my room to find Dad. To ask him to shoot some baskets outside with me.

I found Dad — and Mom — snoozing on the couch in the living room.

I called Ethan and Ray to see if they wanted to

play — but they couldn't. They both had home-work to do.

Tiptoeing through the hall, I left the house through the back door. I stood in the backyard and gazed up at the stars. It was a perfect night. Warm. Not a cloud in the sky.

A perfect night for a short flight over Malibu.

I glanced around — to make sure no one was watching. Then I soared up into the night sky.

Over the rooftops. Over the trees. Over the beach.

I took a deep breath. The ocean air smelled so fresh, so sweet up here.

A light breeze blew through my hair.

So peaceful. So quiet.

So free. Soaring high. Gazing out. Surrounded by nothing but twinkling stars.

I picked up speed. The wind rushed at my face. My T-shirt rippled against my chest.

The stars streamed by. The ocean rolled darkly beneath me.

I gazed down at the Malibu Hills. Then headed toward Los Angeles. I flew over the city. The lights below sparkled for miles.

I flew faster. Barrel-rolled to the left. Then to the right. Then headed into a loop, flying upside down.

Awesome!

Totally awesome!

I'm so lucky! I can sail! Glide! Soar!

"I can FLYYYY!" I whooped, spinning in the air.

I glided for a while on my back, gazing up at the stars. Trying to identify the constellations. Then I spun around and peered down — into total darkness.

No porch lights. No street lamps. No headlights from cars.

No houses. No buildings.

Total darkness.

A wave of panic swept over me. How did this happen? Where is the city? Where am I?

"How long have I been flying?" I groaned. "How far have I flown?"

I didn't know.

I swooped down, searching for a dim light somewhere. But all I saw was darkness. Complete darkness.

I turned around — heading back home, I hoped.

Swooping lower. Searching for a familiar sight.

Finally I spotted a string of lights. A freeway! But *which* freeway? I couldn't tell!

My heart pounded in my chest. Cold beads of sweat prickled my forehead.

I'm lost, I realized, shivering in cold dread.

I am miles and miles from home.

Totally lost.

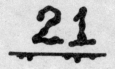

21

I landed in the tall grass on the side of the freeway.

I started to walk. Searching for a sign to tell me where I was.

I walked and walked.

The night was quiet, except for the cars that roared by — and the creepy rustling sounds that escaped from the roadside bushes.

I stared into the bushes. Saw them move.

My heart began to beat faster.

I broke into a jog.

Cars and trucks whirred by me.

A sharp chittering noise rang out from the dense thicket beside the highway. I could see dark eyes glowing in the bushes.

"Hey — !"

A furry creature scuttled across my path.

A raccoon? A skunk?

I started to run.

Up ahead I finally spotted a highway sign.

I ran harder — panting now. Clouds of dirt rose up under my pounding sneakers.

I could see the white letters on the sign — but I still couldn't make out what it said. As I ran toward it, a car pulled alongside me — and stopped.

I spun around — and gasped.

A police cruiser.

Yes! I thought happily. The police! They'll help me get back home.

"Do you need help?" One of the officers stepped out of the squad car. He tipped his cap back and stared into my eyes.

"Yes. I do. I'm kind of lost," I told him breathlessly. "Can you take me home — to Malibu?"

"What is your name?" he asked.

"Jack."

"Well, Jack. You're pretty far from Malibu. How did you get here?" he asked.

I didn't answer. What could I say? I *flew* here? They'd take me back all right. And lock me up — with all the other crazy people in Los Angeles.

"Jack. Did someone drive you here?"

I shook my head no.

"Well, did you just drop out of the sky?" He sounded as if he was losing his patience.

I shrugged my shoulders lamely.

"Get in the car, Jack," the officer nodded toward the car door. "We'll find your parents for you."

Oh, no! I suddenly changed my mind. I can't let

them take me back, I decided, shaking in panic. What will I tell Mom and Dad? How will I explain to them how I got here?

I edged away.

The officer reached out to me. "Get in, Jack. We'll help you."

"Uh . . . no thanks," I told him.

I raised both arms over my head.

And took off.

Gazing down — I saw the other officer leap out of the car.

The two of them stood side by side, gaping up at me with their mouths open wide.

I followed the lights of the highway. I didn't know what else to do. Finally the buildings of Los Angeles came back into view. I let out a long sigh of relief. Then I turned in midair and flew home to Malibu.

I landed quietly behind the garage. I smoothed out my hair. Straightened my T-shirt. I took a deep breath and sneaked into the house.

I could hear my parents in the living room, talking. I stopped in the kitchen and listened.

Were they talking about me?

Did they notice I was gone?

"I don't know where else to look," I heard Dad say. "I've searched everywhere!"

My heart began to pound.

What am I going to tell them?

I held my breath and listened some more.

"I know! I know!" Mom exclaimed. "We have to stay calm. You'll find a new client soon. Someone with real talent. I just know it."

I breathed a long sigh of relief.

They didn't notice.

Next time, I have to be more careful, I promised myself. Much more careful.

Mia is right. Flying can be really dangerous. Especially if you don't know where you're flying!

I tiptoed to my room and closed the door.

The phone rang.

"Are you ready for the big race tomorrow?" It was Wilson.

"Huh? What race?" I asked.

"I told Mr. Grossman that we're going to put on a race for the whole school tomorrow," Wilson declared.

"What kind of race?" I asked him.

"A race they'll never forget!"

22

"Are you crazy?" I yanked Wilson aside in gym class the next morning. "We *can't* race!" I screamed.

"Aw. Come on. Be a good sport." Wilson grinned. "You're just steamed because you know you're going to lose."

On the other side of the gym, I could hear Mr. Grossman announcing the race to the class. "A special race," I heard him say. "Wilson promises we're all in for a big surprise!"

I ran my hand through my hair.

"Wilson, don't you see what you've done?" My voice grew high. "When everyone finds out that we can fly, our lives will be ruined!"

Wilson shrugged, then bent down to tie his sneaker. "I don't know what you're so worried about. This is going to be way cool!"

I glanced around the gym. The empty gym. The entire class had emptied outside, waiting for the race to begin.

"Ready, boys?" Mr. Grossman popped his head in the doorway.

"Ready!" Wilson called back.

Wilson tugged me through the halls. The empty halls.

"Come on, Jack. The whole school is out there!"

The whole school. Out there.

Every kid in Malibu Middle School was going to watch us fly. This was a total disaster.

If we went ahead with this, I knew that my life would never be the same again.

We stepped onto the playground. I squinted in the bright sunlight. Squinted at the crowd of kids, huddled along the running track — waiting for the race to start.

Someone tugged on my T-shirt sleeve.

It was Mia. "Jack, why are you doing this?" she asked, her eyes wide with fear. "Wilson told me you're going to fly."

"I — I don't want to," I stammered. "But I can't do anything about it. I have no choice."

Mia shielded her eyes with her hand and glanced over at Wilson. Her ruby-red heart ring sparkled in the sun.

We both watched Wilson as he stretched out at the starting line. "I'm so worried about the two of you," she said, her eyes locked on Wilson.

I gazed into the crowd.

Kids shifted restlessly from one foot to the other. Watching. Waiting.

91

I wanted to run away.

Run home and hide.

"Hey, Jack!" Ray called out from the crowd. "Go for it! You can beat him!" Ethan stood next to him, pumping his fist in the air.

"Wilson is ready." Mr. Grossman jogged over to me. "How about you, Jack?"

The kids began to chant. "Race! Race! Race!"

My temples were throbbing.

My T-shirt felt wet against my skin — drenched with sweat.

What was I going to do?

23

I had to race.

I knew I had no choice.

I had to race — and I had to win.

I stepped up to Wilson. "Ready, Jackie?" He grinned his horrible Wilson grin.

I nodded.

Mr. Grossman raised the starting flag. "On your marks. Get set. GO!"

Wilson and I took off.

We shot into the air.

With my arms straight out in front of me, I blasted ahead. I soared higher, higher — and zoomed to the other end of the playground, leaving Wilson far behind.

Yes!

I was winning!

Finally!

I was finally beating him!

I turned in midair, dipped, and headed back to

the other end of the playground. I glanced behind me. Wilson was soaring fast. Catching up.

He sailed alongside me. "See you, Jackie!" he smirked. Then he flew ahead.

Oh, no, you don't, Wilson. Not again.

I held my body straight as an arrow — and jetted forward.

We flew side by side now. I could see the muscles in his face straining as he tried to pick up speed.

But he couldn't. He couldn't pull ahead of me.

The other end of the playground was coming up fast. With my eyes trained to the finish line, I soared with all my strength.

We reached the line at the same time. I dropped to the ground. "A tie!" I cried out breathlessly. "It's a tie!"

Wilson hadn't won!

"Hey, Wilson? Wilson?" I searched the school grounds.

Then I glanced up.

There he was, hovering over my head. "Lap number two!" he cried. And took off.

I sprinted into the air.

Too late.

Wilson finished the second lap — and won the race.

"Nice going, Jackie," Wilson clapped me on the shoulder. "I knew I could count on you — to lose!" he hooted.

"That wasn't fair —" I started.

"Hey — what's *their* problem?" he interrupted me, pointing to the crowd of kids.

The quiet crowd.

No cheers.

No clapping.

They stared at us in stunned silence.

I turned to Mr. Grossman. His jaw hung open. He gaped at us — speechless.

I slowly walked over to Ray and Ethan, staring into their unsmiling faces. "So, guys. What did you think?"

"Why didn't you tell us you could fly?" Ray's face broke out into a wide grin.

"I — I wanted to surprise you!" I said, relieved.

"Awesome! Totally awesome!" Ethan shouted. "Can you teach us how?"

"I'm sorry. I can't," I apologized. I told them the whole story — about how I found the book and lost it — as we headed back into school.

"Our basketball team will win every game now!" Ray exclaimed. "Forget about slam dunks! You'll be the first player ever to do a fly-dunk!"

Ray and Ethan were really excited about my flying.

But, later, as I walked to my classroom, I could feel the stares from the other kids. Hear their whispers. Everyone was talking about me. Some shrank back as I approached.

They were afraid of me!

That afternoon, I walked through the halls with my head down. I couldn't stand all the whispers, all the stares.

"Jack!" The school nurse darted from her office and snatched me out of the hall. "There are some people here who want to meet you."

Two men and two women stood stiffly in the nurse's office. One man and one woman were dressed in business suits. The other two wore khaki pants and T-shirts. They smiled warmly at me.

"These people are scientists from the university," the nurse started to explain. "They've heard about your . . . uh . . . special talent. And they want to examine you and Wilson."

I took a step back.

One of the men moved toward me. "If you really can fly, think of how useful you can be to our government — perhaps as a secret weapon against our enemies."

I swallowed hard.

The woman in the khaki pants stuck out her hand. "Come with us, Jack." She shot a nervous glance at the others. "Nothing bad will happen to you."

The others peered at me over their eyeglasses. They nodded eagerly in agreement.

"We just want to look you over. You know. Do a few experiments on you. In our lab."

24

"NO! I don't want to be a lab specimen. I don't want to be a secret weapon!" I shouted at them.

Startled by my cries, the scientists leaped back — and I bolted from the room.

"Jack, come back!" the school nurse called after me.

I raced frantically through the halls. Smashing into kids. Shoving them out of my way.

"Jack, we won't hurt you!" I heard one of the scientists call.

With my head down, I charged ahead, zigzagging through the crowded halls. Elbowing the kids who got in my way.

"Hey, watch it!" Angry voices trailed me as I burst through the school doors and jumped down the steps.

I ran all the way home. I didn't stop. I didn't glance back. I ran hard — even though my lungs felt as if they were about to burst.

I opened my front door with a bang. Then

slammed it shut and leaned against it, gasping for breath.

"Jack?" Dad called from the living room.

Why was Dad home in the middle of the afternoon?

I walked in to the living room — and found both my parents waiting for me.

Dad stood with his hands shoved deep into his pants pockets. "Jack, our phone has been ringing all afternoon," he said sternly. "We heard about you. About what you did in school today."

I glanced over at Mom. She gave a solemn nod.

"You are in a lot of trouble." Dad sounded really really angry now.

I gulped. "Why? What — what are you going to do?"

25

"What do you think we should do, Jack?" Dad paced back and forth in front of me. "We can't believe you didn't tell us sooner."

"Sorry . . ." I muttered. "I mean, I wanted to tell you I could fly. But . . ."

Dad's expression changed. His eyes flashed with excitement. "If you really can fly, you're going to be the hottest act in the country. You're going to be a superstar, Jack. You're going to make millions!"

Mom's face broke into a wide smile.

"We finally found it!" Dad said to her. "I can't believe it. All this time we've been searching everywhere — and it was right under our own roof. We finally found the BIG act!"

"Step right up, ladies and gentlemen! Welcome to the grand opening of Marv's Malibu Motors!" Marvin Milstein stood on a towering platform.

He shouted into a bullhorn, gathering a huge crowd in front of his new car lot.

I stood inside the showroom. I peeked outside — watching the crowd grow. Hundreds of people jammed into the parking lot. Hundreds more tried to shove their way in.

They crammed in tightly. Shoulder to shoulder under the hot sun. And waited.

Waited for me.

The Amazing Flying Boy.

"YES!" Marv continued to shout. "The Amazing Flying Boy is here! In just a moment, you will see him fly over our new shipment of Silver Hawks.

"The Silver Hawk!" Marv pointed across the lot to a shiny, silver car turning slowly on a revolving platform. "The car that soars so smoothly, you'll swear the wheels never touch the ground."

The people packed themselves in tighter — every inch of ground taken up by the crowd.

I could hear the buzz of the crowd over Marv's bullhorn.

"Where is The Flying Boy? Can he really fly?" I heard a little kid cry.

A lump formed in my throat.

Mom came up behind me and placed a hand on my shoulder. "You look great, Jack!"

I stared down at the costume Mom had made for me. A silvery superhero costume. Metallic sneakers. And a shiny silver cape.

"Can you believe this crowd?" Dad exclaimed. "Ten TV stations are out there with their news crews. And tons of reporters — from every newspaper in the state. They're all here to see you, Jack!"

"I don't know, Dad." I stared out at the growing crowd. "Are you sure this is a good idea?"

"A good idea? No. I don't think this is a good idea. It's a *great* idea! It's an *unbelievable* idea!" he cried. "And it's just the start, Jack. Soon you'll have your own TV show. Your own movies. Your own action figures!"

The mob outside grew impatient.

"ARE . . . YOU . . . READY?" Malibu Marv shouted into the bullhorn, pumping up the crowd.

"YES!" Their reply thundered in my ears.

"It's time, Jack!" Dad's eyes lit up with excitement.

I was supposed to fly over the car lot, carrying an advertising banner. Dad handed it to me. It read: FLY WITH THE SILVER HAWK. ONLY AT MALIBU MARV'S.

I stepped outside and climbed the platform steps to take my place next to Marv.

I stared down at the crowd. At their waiting faces. At the doubt in their eyes.

Then I took off.

And the crowd let out a startled gasp.

I flew around the lot carrying the banner, staring down at the people as they gaped up at me.

"He's flying! He's really flying!" I heard someone shout.

I searched the faces below — trying to find Mia, Ethan, or Ray. I hadn't seen them in days. I soared around the entire car lot, but I couldn't spot them in the crowd.

"You're seeing a miracle, folks!" Marv's amplified voice floated up to me. "And our Silver Hawk prices are a miracle, too!"

The next morning, Dad brought in reporters from *Time* and *Newsweek* to interview me. The reporters asked me tons of questions: When did you learn to fly? Can you teach other kids how to do it? What was in the secret recipe you ate? What were the magic words you chanted? Then their photographers snapped pictures of me flying around the backyard.

People and *TV Guide* showed up next. They asked the same questions. Took the same pictures.

Mia called. She asked me to go skating with her that afternoon. I wanted to go, but I couldn't. Someone from the *Wall Street Journal* was coming to interview me.

I wanted to tell them to talk to *TV Guide* — get the answers from them. But I knew Mom and Dad wouldn't like that. They were working really hard to get me all these interviews.

"See you later!" I called to Mom and Dad the

next morning. I was going to the park to shoot some hoops with Ray and Ethan.

"Whoa! Wait up!" Dad charged in to the kitchen. "Where are you going?"

"To play basketball with my friends. I won't be home late," I told him.

"Sorry, Jack. But you can't go."

"Why not?" I asked, confused. "I don't have any interviews today."

"Because basketball isn't the right kind of exercise for a flying superhero!" Dad patted me on the back. "You have to do sit-ups, push-ups, run some laps — build up your strength and stamina to fly your best!"

He pushed me toward the door. "You have to work out every day, Jack. Every day. Now, let's get started. I'll work with you in the backyard."

I didn't see Ray or Ethan or Mia that whole week. I had more interviews to do. And exercises. And costume fittings. And I did a flying appearance at the opening of a new restaurant in Santa Monica.

Finally Saturday arrived. Mom and Dad said it was my day off. No interviews. No exercises. No jobs. I could do whatever I wanted.

I got up early to go Rollerblading with Mia. As I headed out the door, Mom stopped me. "Jack, you can't go out like *that*!"

"Like what?" I asked, staring down at my T-shirt and cutoff jeans.

103

"Like that," she said, pointing to my clothes. "You're a superstar now. You have to wear your flying costume when you go out. So your fans won't be disappointed."

"But, Mom!" I protested. "I can't wear my cape to go skating. No way I'm going to wear silver tights in the park!"

I called Mia and told her I couldn't go. I shuffled glumly into the living room and turned on the TV.

I knew that flying in front of the whole school was a big mistake.

I knew it would ruin my life. I knew it!

I hadn't seen my friends in weeks. I'd probably never see them again!

I'm going to spend my whole life flying around in a dumb costume, never having any fun! I realized.

I flipped aimlessly through the channels.

I flipped and flipped, watching the programs flash by on the screen.

And then I stopped — when I saw Wilson. Wilson on TV!

Wilson — wearing a really cool superhero costume that sparkled with neon glitter.

My eyes grew wide as I watched him. He soared around a mountaintop, rescuing people off its steep cliffs.

"We will return to *Wonder Wilson and His*

Amazing Rescues in just a moment!" the TV announcer said.

Huh? *Wonder Wilson and His Amazing Rescues?*

I shook my head.

"I'm doing restaurant openings — and Wilson already has his own TV show!" I wailed.

Can't I EVER beat Wilson? EVER?

I heard a knock on the door. I was glad to leave the room before *Wonder Wilson* came back on TV.

I opened the door — and saw three serious-looking men in green uniforms standing there. Army uniforms.

"Jack Johnson?" one of them asked sternly.

I nodded yes.

"Good." He reached out his hand. "You'll have to come with us."

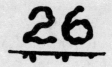

26

I stood in the middle of a drab green room.

An army lab.

With no windows.

The room smelled like a doctor's office. You know. That heavy alcohol smell.

I glanced over at the door. A solid steel bolt sealed it shut.

A chair with suction cups stuck all over the back and seat stood in one corner of the room. Electrical wires streamed from each cup.

I imagined that was what a prison electric chair looked like. No way I'd ever sit on it!

My heart began to pound as a group of army scientists in white lab coats circled me. They stared at me, their eyes moving up and down my body. They wrote on clipboards they held in their hands. Then they stared at me some more.

"Okay, Jack. We are going to perform a few tests. Are you ready?" one of the scientists asked.

"No!" I shouted. "I am not ready. I want to go home!"

"Sorry, Jack," the scientist said. "We can't let you go just yet. Now — please come with us."

They led me outside to a wide courtyard. The courtyard was covered with canvas. I felt as if I were in an enormous circus tent.

As soon as we were closed in, the scientists began shouting commands at me:

Fly on your back.

Fly on your belly.

Fly with your eyes closed.

Fly with your legs crossed.

Hold your breath and fly. Hold your ears and fly. Hold your thoughts and fly.

They ordered me to fly a thousand different ways.

They wouldn't stop.

They wouldn't let me rest until I was panting like a dog.

One scientist handed me a bottle of cold water. He motioned for me to sit down on the ground. They formed a circle around me.

"Okay, Jack," another scientist said. "Time for some questions. First tell us — how long have you been flying?"

Same questions — all over again.

"Only for a few weeks," I replied.

All the scientists scribbled down my answer.

"How did you learn to fly?" he asked.

"Didn't you guys read *Time* or *Newsweek* or *TV Guide*?" I asked.

"Just answer the question, Jack," the scientist said sternly.

"I ate a special formula," I answered, rolling my eyes impatiently.

The scientists' heads jerked up from their clipboards. "What was in the special formula?"

"I don't remember," I replied.

"Yes, you do, Jack." The scientist stepped closer to me. He stared hard into my eyes. "Now tell us."

I thought hard, trying to recall what was in the recipe. But I couldn't. "I — I really don't remember," I stammered.

"Think harder, Jack," he demanded. "You know what was in it. Tell us."

My heart pounded in my chest. "I — I don't remember. I'm telling you the truth. I really don't remember."

The scientists didn't believe me. They waited. Stared at me with unblinking eyes. Waiting for my answer.

I peered down at my sneakers to escape their hard stares.

Where were my parents? Did they know I was here?

I could feel a bead of sweat trickle down my back.

"Please, let me go!" I begged.

"Sorry, Jack," one of the scientists said. "First you have to answer the question."

"But I can't! I told you — I don't remember!" I cried.

"Okay. Then we'll move on," the scientist said. The others nodded in agreement.

I let out a sigh of relief.

"Jack — we're going back in there." The scientist led me to the little room. "Now — sit in that chair."

"Huh? What are you going to do to me?" I asked.

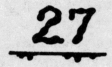

27

More questions.

Then more flying demonstrations.

Then they hooked me up to the suction cups on the chair. That was the worst.

It measured how fast my heart beat. How fast my pulse raced. How fast my eyes blinked. Hours and hours of measuring the slightest movements in my body. Down to a slight twitch.

Then they shut me up in a metal tank and took some kind of laser pictures of me.

Then they asked more questions.

Ten hours later, Dad sat next to me on the living room couch, apologizing. "I'm really sorry, Jack. They gave us no choice. They said you had to go with them. But they didn't tell us it would take so long."

Dad sighed. "I was so busy getting you flying jobs, I forgot to warn you they were coming. But forget about all that, Jack. I have great news. I've set up the race of a lifetime."

"Race? What kind of a race?" I demanded.

"A race between you and Wilson!" Dad exclaimed. "The Amazing Flying Boy races Wonder Wilson — your first appearance together! The winner will receive a million dollars! Just think of it, Jack. ONE MILLION DOLLARS!"

"A million dollars?" I couldn't believe it.

"The race will be on TV all around the world." Dad stood and began pacing. "Two billion people will be watching."

Wow. A million dollars! And everyone in the world will see me fly like a superhero. And Wilson and I will become the two most famous kids on earth!

This really was *awesome*!

"And if you win the race, son — it will be worth billions of dollars!" Dad's hands flew up in the air as he talked. "Think of the TV commercials you'll make! You'll be a star all around the world!"

I slowly got up from the couch. "I — I have to go out for a walk, Dad. I need some time to think about all of this."

I walked down the block, thinking about everything Dad said.

"Hey, there's The Amazing Flying Boy!" someone shouted from a passing car.

"That's him! There he is! The kid who flies!"

Shouts from other cars now. People pointing. Cheering. Waving. From almost every car that drove by.

111

I walked faster. With my head down.

"Malibu Motors Flying Boy! Marv's flying kid!" More shouts. "The flying Johnson kid!"

I heard footsteps behind me.

I glanced back. A group of kids were following me. I started to jog.

"Flying Boy! Slow down!" They began chasing me. "Fly for us! Come on, take off. Fly around the block!"

I broke into a run. I ducked behind some bushes until they passed. Then I walked some more — keeping in the shadows.

I am going to be the most famous kid on earth, I thought, trying to cheer myself up.

I am going to race in front of two billion people — and then my life will never be the same again. I am going to be rich and famous.

Rich and famous.

My stomach tightened. All my muscles tensed. Can I do it?

Can I race in front of two billion people?

And most important — *can I finally beat Wilson?*

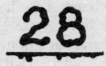

28

The day of the big race.

Mom, Dad, and I rode to the bottom of the Hollywood Hills. That's where the race would begin.

Wilson and I would take off from there. Then fly up to the HOLLYWOOD sign. Then back down again.

Dad inched our car up to the grandstand.

Thousands of people had turned out to watch Wilson and me fly.

Thousands of people watched as our car drove up.

Their hands pressed against the car. Their staring eyes gawked at me through the windows. A mass of bodies and faces inching along with us. So many people, they blocked out the sunlight.

I sat in the backseat in darkness.

Staring at the faces gaping in at me.

Listening to their shouts.

That's him! He's here!

Are you nervous?

Can we talk to you before the race?
What did you eat for breakfast?
What are you going to do with all the money?
Will you come to our school and fly?
Are you from another planet?

"Hey!" Someone banged on the window — and I jumped. "Can I have your autograph?" He banged again. I shrank back in my seat.

"Pretty exciting, huh?" Dad smiled in the rearview mirror.

Jack, we love you! Jack, you're amazing! Jack — teach me how to fly! Cries rang out all around me.

Dad parked the car.

The crowd pressed against the doors. Sealing us in. The car started to rock under their weight.

My heart began to pound.

I grabbed onto the seat so tightly my knuckles turned white.

"Coming through. Stand aside." A troop of policemen cleared a path to the car.

The officers opened the door.

I didn't move.

"Let's go, Jack. It's time!" Dad said.

On shaky legs, I stepped out of the car. A deafening roar rose up from the crowd.

"Jack. Jack. Jack." The chant thundered in my ears.

The policemen formed a barricade, holding the shouting, cheering, chanting people back. I made

114

my way to a big concrete platform built especially for the race.

Arms reached out — reached out to touch me. Hands grabbed at my sleeves. Grabbed at my cape. Grabbed. Grabbed frantically. Pulled me toward them.

I struggled to walk. To pull free of the grasping hands.

The policemen tried to hold the crowd back — but people surged forward in a heavy wave.

They broke through the policemen's barrier.

Pressed against me.

Started to crush me.

I was drowning. Drowning in hands and legs and talking faces. A wave of panic washed over me.

I lost Mom and Dad in the sea of bodies.

The crowd swept over me. Carried me with it.

Jack! Jack! Jack! They shouted my name over and over.

"Mom! Dad!" I tried to cry out over the roar of the mob.

I couldn't see.

I couldn't breathe.

I gasped for air.

I — I'm not going to make it, I realized.

The crowd — it's *swallowing* me. Swallowing me up . . .

29

Then I felt someone grab me under my shoulders. "This way, Jack." Two policemen guided me up the platform steps. Four other dark-uniformed officers surrounded me.

When I reached the top, I took a deep breath — and gazed out at the people. Thousands of people — stretching out for miles and miles.

"Jack!" Someone shoved a microphone in my face.

"Jack! Over here." Another microphone.

Jack! Jack! Jack! Hundreds of microphones suddenly appeared before me.

Cameras clicked. "Do you think you can win?" a reporter demanded.

"I —"

"When did you learn to fly?" Another reporter.

"Three months —"

"What was in the secret recipe?" Another reporter.

Everyone asking questions — all at once. Cameras clicking.

JACK! JACK! JACK! Everyone calling to me.

I broke into a heavy, cold sweat.

I tugged at the collar of my silver costume. Choking, I thought. It's . . . choking me.

The mob of people continued to call out my name.

And Wilson's name.

I glanced over to the other side of the platform.

There he was. Wilson — in his glittering superhero outfit. Hands planted on his hips. Chest puffed out. Laughing with the newspaper reporters. Smiling for the magazine writers. Boasting to the TV cameras.

He LOVES this! I realized. How could he? How could anyone like this?

"We are about to begin," the announcer said to me as he waved Wilson over.

"This is it." Wilson clapped me on the back. "I'm really sorry, Jackie."

"Sorry for what?" I asked.

"Sorry to have to beat you in front of two billion people!" he hooted. "Good luck, Jackie. You'll need it."

A striped-shirted referee asked us to shake hands before the race.

I shook Wilson's hand — and tried to crush his

fingers. But Wilson just grinned his horrible Wilson grin.

"The race is about to begin!" The announcer's voice boomed over the enormous loudspeaker.

The crowd had been roaring. But now the roar faded to a whisper of hushed voices.

The referee lifted a starter's pistol.

I took a deep breath — and held it.

I shut my eyes — and waited to hear the blast from the gun.

BANG!

30

The gunshot echoed in my ears.

I opened my eyes in time to watch Wilson take off. His cape swirled behind him as he lifted toward the sky.

I raised my arms.

I leaped into the air.

And landed hard on my feet.

A shocked gasp rose up from the crowd.

I raised my arms again. They trembled as I pointed them to the sky.

I bent my knees. Then took a strong leap.

And landed with a loud *thud* on the concrete platform.

I could hear the gasps of the crowd. I could see their open mouths, their wide eyes. Stunned. They were all stunned.

I tried again.

Nothing.

I glanced up to see Wilson soaring high, nearing the big HOLLYWOOD sign.

"I — I can't fly!" I cried out. "I can't fly anymore. I've lost it! It's gone!"

Dad jumped onto the stage. His face was frantic. "Try again! Try, Jack! Keep trying!"

I took a long, deep breath.

I planted my feet together.

I bent my knees and with all my might — I sprang up.

And came down.

Nothing.

No use.

"I've lost it!" I cried. "I can't fly anymore! I can't fly!"

I gazed up and saw Wilson soar over the HOLLYWOOD sign, turn, and start back.

Wilson wins again, I told myself. Wilson wins again.

31

As the summer passed, we didn't see much of Wilson. He was busy flying all the time. His TV show was on every week. And he made dozens of flying appearances all over the country.

In the fall, he had to leave Malibu Middle School because he was always traveling. Always making flying appearances. Always working, working. On the run.

I saw on the TV news that the army follows him wherever he goes, doing experiments on him. Trying to figure out how to get other people to fly.

When Wilson is home, he's too tired to see his old friends. Mia says it doesn't matter. She says hanging out with me is much more fun.

I'm back to my old normal life. Morty is too. He finally came out of his doghouse. And he doesn't float off the ground anymore — not since I tied a two-pound dog tag to his collar.

Ethan and Ray and I are going to a Lakers

game tonight. And tomorrow, Mia invited me to go to a Purple Rose concert with her. Next weekend we're taking tennis lessons together.

We never talk about the big race and how Wilson won.

We never talk about flying at all.

I've kept my secret from Mia. I've kept my secret from everyone.

I've never told *anyone* that I can still fly.

And I've never told anyone that I only *pretended* to lose my flying ability that morning of the race.

Yes. You heard me. I only pretended.

I *let* Wilson win the race.

Why?

Because I knew that was the only way I could win.

That was the only way I could get all those thousands of people out of my life. It was the only way I could get my friends back. The only way I could get my normal life back. The only way I could be happy.

I told you. I'm not the kind of kid who likes to enter contests. I don't like to compete. I don't care about winning.

So, I'm really lucky. Because even though I don't care about winning — I won after all.

Sometimes, very late at night, I sneak out of the house. And I fly over Malibu, high over the ocean. I gaze down on the waves sparkling in the moonlight. I soar with the winds and sail up toward the moon, feeling the cool ocean breezes on my face.

And I think about how lucky I am.

And how smart.

And I wish Wonder Wilson a lot of luck.

Really. . . .

Add *more*

to your collection . . .

Here's a chilling preview of

THE BLOB THAT ATE EVERYONE

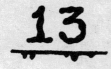

13

Alex and I both gaped at the empty spot on the front of my desktop. Alex pushed up her glasses and squinted.

"It — it's gone," I murmured weakly. My knees started to buckle. I grabbed my dresser to hold myself up.

"Weird," Alex muttered, shaking her head. "Are you sure —"

"It just disappeared into thin air!" I interrupted. "I don't *believe* this! How? How could it disappear?"

"How could *what* disappear?" a voice called from the doorway.

I whirled around — to see Dad lumber heavily into the room. He carried the old typewriter in his arms.

"Dad — why . . . ?" I started.

He set it down on the desk. Then he pushed his curly black hair off his forehead and grinned at me. "I cleaned it for you, Zackie," he said. "And put in a new ribbon."

He wiped sweat off his forehead with the back of his hand. "Ribbons are hard to find these days," he added. "No one uses typewriters anymore."

Alex laughed. "Zackie thought the typewriter disappeared into thin air!"

I flashed Alex an angry look. "Alex — give me a break," I whispered.

She made a face at me.

Dad shook his head. "It's a little too heavy to disappear into thin air," he sighed. "It weighs a ton! More than a computer!"

I walked over to the typewriter and ran my hands over the smooth, dark metal. "Thanks for cleaning it up, Dad," I said. "It looks awesome."

"A few of the keys were sticking," Dad added. "So I oiled them up. I think the old machine is working fine now, Zackie. You should be able to write some great stories on it."

"Thanks, Dad," I repeated.

I couldn't wait to get started. I reached into my top drawer for some paper. Then I noticed that Dad hadn't left. He was lingering by the door, watching Alex and me.

"Your mom went across the street to visit Janet Hawkins, our new neighbor," he said. "It's such a beautiful spring night. I thought maybe you two would like to take a walk into town to get some ice cream."

"Uh . . . no thanks," Alex replied. "I already had dessert at home. Before I came over."

"And I really want to get started typing my new scary story," I told him.

He sighed and looked disappointed. I think he really wanted an excuse to get ice cream.

As soon as he left, I dropped into my desk chair. I slid a fresh, white sheet of paper into the typewriter roller.

Alex pulled up a chair and sat beside me. "Can I try the typewriter after you?" she asked.

"Yes. *After* me," I replied impatiently.

I really wanted to get my story typed.

I let my eyes wander over the round, black keys. Then I leaned forward and started to type.

Typing on a typewriter is a lot different from typing on a keyboard. For one thing, you have to press the keys a lot harder.

It took me a few tries to get the feel of the thing.

Then I typed the first words of the story:

IT WAS A DARK AND STORMY NIGHT.

"Hey —!" I uttered a cry as lightning flashed in my bedroom window.

Rain pounded on the glass.

A sharp roar of thunder shook the house.

Darkness swept over me as all the lights went out.

"Zackie —?" Alex cried in a tiny voice. "Zackie? Zackie? Are you all right?"

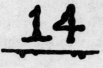

14

I swallowed hard. "Yes. I'm okay," I said quietly.

Alex is the only person in the world who knows that I'm afraid of the dark.

I'm afraid of mice. And I'm afraid of the dark. I admit it.

And I'm afraid of a lot of other things.

I'm afraid of big dogs. I'm afraid of going down to the basement when I'm all alone in the house. I'm afraid of jumping into the deep end of the swimming pool.

I've told Alex about some of my fears. But not all of them.

I mean, it's kind of embarrassing.

Why do I write scary stories if I'm afraid of so many things?

I don't know. Maybe I write better stories because I know what being scared feels like.

"The lights went off so suddenly," Alex said. She stood beside me, leaning over my desk to see out the window. "Usually they flicker or something."

Sheets of rain pounded against the windowpane. Jagged streaks of lightning crackled across the sky.

I stayed in my desk chair, gripping the arms tightly. "I'm glad Adam isn't here," I murmured. "He'd just make fun of me."

"But you're not very scared now — are you?" Alex asked.

An explosion of thunder made me nearly jump out of the chair.

"A little," I confessed.

And then I heard the footsteps. Heavy, thudding footsteps from out in the hall.

Thunder roared again.

I spun away from the window. And listened to the footsteps, thudding heavily on the carpet.

"Who's there?" I called through the darkness.

I saw a flicker of yellow light in the doorway. A shadow swept over the wallpaper in the hall.

Dad stepped into the room. "This is so weird," he said. He was carrying two candles in candlesticks. Their flames bent and nearly went out as he carried them to my desk.

"Where did that storm come from?" Dad asked, setting the candles beside my typewriter. "Are you okay, Zackie?"

I forgot. Dad also knows I'm scared of the dark.

"I'm fine," I told him. "Thanks for the candles."

Dad stared out the window. We couldn't really see anything out there. The rain was coming down too hard.

"The sky was clear a few seconds ago," Dad said, leaning over me to get a better view. "I can't believe such a big storm could blow in so quickly."

"It's weird," I agreed.

We stared at the rain for a minute or so. Sheets of lightning made the backyard glow like silver.

"I'm going to call your mother," Dad said. "I'm going to tell her to wait out the storm." He patted me on the back, then headed to the door.

"Don't you want a candle?" I called after him.

"No. I'll find my way," he replied. "I have a flashlight in the basement." He disappeared down the hall.

"What do you want to do now?" Alex asked. Her face looked orange in the candlelight. Her eyes glowed like cat eyes.

I turned back to the typewriter. "It would be cool to write by candlelight," I said. "Scary stories should *always* be written by candlelight. I'll bet that's how all the famous horror writers write their stories."

"Cool," Alex replied. "Go ahead."

I slid the candlesticks closer. The yellow light flickered over the typewriter keys.

I leaned forward and read over the first sentence of my story:

IT WAS A DARK AND STORMY NIGHT.

Then I hit the space bar and typed the next sentence:

THE WIND BEGAN TO HOWL.

I hit the space bar again. And raised my fingers to type the next sentence.

But a rattling noise made me jump.

"What is *that*?" I gasped.

"The window." Alex pointed.

Outside, the wind blew hard, rattling the windowpane.

Over the steady roar of the rain, I heard another sound. A strange howl.

I gripped the arms of my desk chair. "Do you hear that?" I asked Alex.

She nodded. Her eyes squinted out the window.

"It's just the wind," she said softly. "It's howling through the trees."

Outside, the howling grew louder as the wind swirled around my house. The window rattled and shook.

The howling grew high and shrill, almost like a human voice, a human wail.

I felt a chill run down my back.

Gripping the chair arms tightly, I struggled to keep my fear down.

It's just a storm, I told myself. Just a rainstorm. Just a lot of rain and wind.

I glanced at the words I had typed. In the flickering, orange light, the black type jumped out at me:

THE WIND BEGAN TO HOWL.

I listened to the shrill howl outside. It seemed to surround me, surround the house.

"How strange," I muttered.

And then, things got a lot stranger.